One of the things I learned
fantastic episodes you read
novel are usually the ones drawn most directly
from life. What appears exaggeration can easily be
a toning down of the original event and what
appears to be most ordinary is frequently complete
invention. It is a talent few writers (even fewer of
them living) have and I admire it considerably. At
his best, Jack Story has a fluently innovative
technique which has evolved quite a bit since *The
Trouble with Harry* and which was evolving pretty
radically from *I Sit in Hanger Lane* through *One
Last Mad Embrace* (another H.S. Fenton story),
*Hitler Needs You*, *The Wind in the Snottygobble
Tree* etc.

There can't be many writers who won't feel
sympathy (or even total empathy) with Jack's
description of what life is like working for the
movies. He captures the essence of it. It always
drives you crazy. The debts and the habit of
spending fabulous sums before they are actually
concrete is something else most of us have ex-
perienced, in common with every other sort of
artist, criminal and small-time entrepreneur in the
world. The desperate half-baked schemes for con-
fusing creditors, the horrible confusion between
wanting to work and having to run/cook the supper/
tend to the sick/visit your mother, the destructive
lure of a regular job; all these are the real world of the
writer's life, very rarely touched on by anyone. Jack
Trevor Story is one of those brave spirits willing to
risk being branded a renegade, willing to spill the
beans, to show the horrible truth of the average
fictioneer's day-to-day life. He is also one of the first
to describe what some dignify as 'alienation' but
what is actually a common dilemma of writers called:
*How to appear normal* (see Page 124).

This book was not a bestseller when it first came out. I don't think it would have made much difference to Jack if it had been. As he once told a judge at a bankruptcy hearing (when the judge wanted to know how he had managed to get through such a large sum of money in such a short time): 'You know how it is, Judge, twenty or two hundred, it always lasts a week to a fortnight.' The chances are, however, that it will eventually (together with the other Horace books) be turned into an excellent movie. There was a rumour a little while ago that another film company wanted to do it. They had heard that the largest film audiences were in India and that it might be possible to get money from producers there. It meant that the book had to be rejigged a bit. The script would now be set in Calcutta, Horace would be leaving a posthumous account of his life, having decided to end it all. It would be called, of course, *I Hang in Sitar Lane*. Luckily, the chance to write a *Doctor Who* serial came up before Jack had to consider shelving his principles. I hope one day we will see Horace's adventures on the screen – they'd make a marvellous TV series. Meanwhile, you have this book. Treasure it. It's one of the funniest, most humane, most truthful books published anywhere for a long time.

Michael Moorcock

Jack Trevor Story

# I SIT IN
# HANGER LANE

ALLISON & BUSBY

An Allison & Busby book
Published in 1990 by
W. H. Allen & Co. PLC
Unit 26, Grand Union Centre,
338 Ladbroke Grove
London W10 5AH

Copyright © 1968 by Jack Trevor Story

Printed in Great Britain by
Cox & Wyman Ltd, Reading

ISBN 0 74900 097 X

# Chapters

TO THE MEMORY
OF A DEAD FRIEND

# 1

# The Girl

I sit in Hanger Lane
I used to think it was an escape route but now I suspect
it was a short cut to the womb. I see they've finished the
under-pass. I sneaked up there tonight on my way back from
town and parked in a service road for half an hour watching
the traffic lights I used to cross. The roads of my life have
always fascinated me. The way the most familiar ones, sometimes separated by half a lifetime and God knows how many
people and dramas, you now discover because of a diversion,
run within yards of each other. Or that two roads you use all
the time turn out to be the same road travelled in the opposite direction. I am always being amazed by these chance
encounters with roads that happened years ago.

The girl was awake when I got back and crying to go to
the lavatory. It was just bitchiness, she could have done it
in the plastic bowl. The walls are so close together and the
furniture is so tight-packed she can lift herself around fairly
comfortably when she's in the mood.

"Where've you been?"

She was sniffing my coat and looking for woman-signs as
I carried her down the site. I told her I'd been to borrow ten
pounds from my agent. He had lent me fifty. Not all in cash.
He had paid the caravan rent arrears, brought Tres's and
Edna's (my two wives) payments up to date, given me
enough to get a pair of shoes in case there was someone to

see in television. His secretary had given me a cup of tea and asked me if I was all right.

When you go in they move swiftly and quietly into action like those people who used to help the resistance fighters in the days of enemy occupation; calm reassuring words but not too many, no questions about the fighting.

"There's a new television series coming up—he says they want me."

Always ready with the white lie to boost your morale no matter some script editor has just said he won't touch you with a bargepole after the way you infiltrated your fascist propaganda into some peak-viewing hour.

"I see," she said.

This meant she was planning to go into it more thoroughly when she was in a more advantageous position. Her love-making was full of advantageous positions; she had me in the palm of her hand and that's not all. We came to the concrete bunkers, the bogs, and I carried her inside, thankful for the dark.

"That's about the closest thing I've seen to Quasimodo carrying Esmerelda into Notre Dame," Tony told me the first time he saw it happen (I am more than twice her age but not hunchbacked). He's a trombone player, also cast away, probably.

The girl, daughter of a landed family, hung on to the door trying to keep her feet out of the puddles of urine while I cleaned the pottie-effluent off the seat and covered it with the *Evening Standard*. I got her seated and gave her toilet paper in blue (we used to make jokes about the colour and texture in terms of the ethereal commercials, light as gossamer and hygienic too, but they wore out).

"Don't listen!" she called.

This defenceless plea always touched me deeply. How could I ever leave her? I waited outside but the sound carried just as clearly although I knew she was trying to keep it down; this makes you more emotionally protective about people than do all their artifices of vanity.

[8]

In case you got the idea that the caravan site is idyllic in any way it's not. There is a central Motel with all its corrupt and decadent twentieth-century implication; fifty caravans all different, all with bits of yard or garden or grass and little fences and post-boxes and clothes-lines pretending to be real houses; a big pyramidical black ash-tip, a car-breaking yard, the ruins of greenhouses and radiators, all criss-crossed with power lines on posts running at head height and monumented with the aerial sculpture of TV aerials pulling the miracle down to earth. Nobody waking up here would believe there had not been an atomic war.

"Ready," she called.

I went in and lifted her off, pulled the chain for her without looking down the pan, held my breath until we got outside.

"Did you see the new poem?" she asked.

I had seen it, written on the whitewashed wall with a finger dipped in something brown.

> *The Wilsons are having an orgy,*
> *The caravan's rocking like mad,*
> *Mrs Wilson is stuck to the Corgi*
> *And Betty's in bed with her dad.*

It was quite a witty blow in one of the camp feuds. I noticed as we went back that all my stars were out. I have six.

"Swear you didn't go to see any of your kids," she said when I was washing her in the sink.

I swore it.

She wouldn't have any babies now was more than half the trouble.

"And here," she said.

I washed her there.

"Petal," she said.

Or flower or blossom. I was forgiven and it was time for bed. I admire writers who manage to make sexual intercourse palpitate but I've got some kind of block. It's not that it's not important it's too important. I can't conduct a racy conversation about my main spring.

"It must be terrible to finish with that side of life at her age," kind people said.

This meant do you still lie on top of that poor crippled child and penetrate her?

"The television must be a great comfort to her," they said.

This meant does she still have orgasms?

My first sexual experience was with a stench pole in the Castle Grounds at Hertford. It was nineteen-twenty-one, I was four years old and Scott Fitzgerald had already published *This Side of Paradise.* Hemingway I believe was in Paris. I was late already. I also admire writers who can talk tersely about their tough under-privileged childhood but I have to admit that we were just sliding down this stench pole. The other children did it a lot but I didn't see the point of it until one day I lost them and climbed the pole to see if I could spot them. When I slid down I believe is when all my troubles started. It was dark when they came looking for me and I was still doing it.

What happened in my loins then was still happening now with the girl. I'm hoping it happens until you're ninety.

"Where did you go?" she asked me.

To get the truth she would hold me in her mouth the way a cat holds a kitten, completely powerless and with the possibility of having its head bitten off.

I told her.

"You want to leave me, don't you, Horace?" she said, afterwards.

She didn't want the truth this time and didn't get it.

"You're not happy," she said. "You're not as happy as you were when you were miserable all the time. With all your moaning you had a lilt in your voice. You enjoyed it."

Old Angie was right. She always said it wasn't me. She said I'd chosen completely the wrong kind of women. Then when she met the girl for the first time she said, grieving for me and nearly crying:

[10]

"You've done it again, Horace!"

Not quite, Angie. Not this.

This time I am marooned on a desert island and my distress signals are being misunderstood or purposely ignored. An aeroplane comes over in the dark hours of the morning and I signal an SOS with the door lamp that hangs on the caravan rain gutter. Yesterday I saw my eldest daughter Lang cross the road. She didn't know it was me and I hadn't the courage it would take to break the news.

The girl has dressed me in old clothes that belonged to her brother. Tight striped jeans that waiters wear, a zipped suedette windcheater, sandals without socks, various worn-out shirts. My hair is down on my shoulders now and I have a beard. Children on the site call me old Ben Gunn. Nice to know that they read.

Last night the aeroplane engine seemed to cut out directly overhead while I was flashing the lamp. I went out in my pyjamas and looked up but could see nothing. Spanish Manuella appeared out of the trees.

"Very good weather!" he laughed.

At first you think Manuella is speaking perfect English but he's learned all the weather clichés and nothing else. "It is wanted!" he will shout. Or: "I think it will pass over!"

Later I heard a nightingale singing. I can write fairly leisurely about this kind of thing. If she thinks I'm writing about my life, my families, the film business, girls, she makes life hell. I walked into the woods and came upon Manuella whistling beautifully, his fingers in his mouth. It wasn't a nightingale, it was him.

"The farmers need it!" he laughed.

I fit in here. I wondered about places like this when I was driving my roads. About people who seemed to have dropped out of the race. Was it tragedy, engine trouble, or were they just short of breath? They can get away, of course. We all can. But where would we go?

You are cast away whether you are on a desert island or on the mainland with the rest of your world on a desert island.

# 2

# Albert

"Let me talk to him," Albert said.

"It wouldn't do any good," I told him.

He had seen me withering through the summer, working on a film that seemed fated not to go through. I had two wives, eight children, seventeen cats, dozens of rats and mice, a hedgehog, a squirrel, a hundred or so creditors, my bank manager, all waiting for it to go through.

"Let me be your manager," Albert said. "On the film side."

He was a milkman.

We had called in a pub, looking for girls. We hadn't found any again.

"Money, money, money," Albert said. "I'm not going to think about anything else from now on and you shouldn't either."

He made it sound like a new project.

"Would either of you gentlemen like a raffle ticket?" the landlord asked us.

Albert cross-examined him about the raffle. Whether he got a rake-off, what the prizes cost, how much was the printing, how many tickets did they expect to sell.

"You put your right name, stupid!" he told me when I'd bought a ticket.

He had a cloak and dagger mood. Then he'd have a mood where he'd piss his right name on a lavatory wall and walk away proud. I've seen him flash a badge at a railway collector instead of his ticket.

"Why did you do that?" I asked him.

"It scares shit out of them," Albert said.

I started by owing him money for milk. My reasons for not being able to pay kept him on the doorstep for hours. He started coming round in the evenings to hear more. I was show business. I should be in Park Lane or Hollywood.

"You're doing it all wrong, mate," Albert said.

He got me to change my family Morris for an Armstrong Siddeley Hurricane coupé that let in the rain. He put me through a course of check shirts and bow ties, a green grey suit made by one of his customers to his specifications; tapered trousers, turn-back cuffs, draped back and hand-stitched lapels. Tres, a homely woman of fifty (he was always trying to get me to change her) refused to go out with me in it. Lewis and Fiona stopped asking me to meet them out of school.

"You've got to think about your image," Albert said.

It didn't do me any good locally with tradesmen and people I owed money to. They thought I was flashing it and not giving them any. Being a writer in that kind of community was something you had to live down, not up. He got me on the stage of the local cinema when one of my pictures was showing then criticised me afterwards.

"People don't want to hear about your money troubles," Albert said.

He produced Diana.

A film I had written was going to have a Royal Première in the West End. It was not the kind of thing I would normally go to. It meant hiring a dinner suit.

"We're going to do this properly," Albert said.

He turned up at the house in a blue suit and wearing his milkman's cap with the dairy name hidden by a piece of black insulating tape. He had got Diana to lie full-length on the back seat of the car so that Tres wouldn't see her.

"Head for Hanger Lane," I told him.

It was Edna's housekeeping-money day. Albert was angry.

"I've done my part," he told Diana. "Now you watch him do his."

However unspectacular the rest of the evening our arrival outside my council house must have gratified Albert a little and repaid him for his trouble. It brought the neighbours out and Edna with them. It was Albert's triumph. He had worked hard on all of us. I looked handsome in a dinner suit, Diana was beautiful the way a Christmas Tree is beautiful and the Hurricane drophead gleaming in two-shades of lovat green is an aristocrat.

Edna watched the exhibition for a moment with the rest, forgetting that she was married to it. She was taking pins out of her hair, hurriedly, putting them into her mouth, chatting to the woman next door.

"I inarf late," she said, coming to the car as I got out.

I gave her her money and told her about the première.

"Could you pop me off on the way?" she said.

Albert did the deadpan thing of looking at her and then at me and then at Diana and then panning away to infinity.

"Is that your mother?" Diana asked, politely.

"That's his secret life," Albert said. "You should *see* his mother."

Edna had scuttled in and scuttled out with her office-cleaning overall. "Can I sit in the front?" she asked.

As she got in my eldest daughter came to the gate holding her child. I greeted her, kissed her, said goodbye.

"Say goodbye to grandad!" she told the child.

Albert shuddered.

We dropped Edna at her office-cleaning job and I borrowed enough back for three gallons of petrol.

We arrived at the cinema too late for the royal handshaking. Albert got back from parking the car and pushed his way through to the public side of the scarlet ropes. The guards band in plumed helmets was playing the theme tune from the film. The royal party was shaking hands with

[14]

Arturo Conti, the producer-director, and the stars. Diana and I had been hastily hidden in an alcove and a photographer was giving me his burnt-out flash-bulbs.

"Go on!" Albert shouted. "Get in line!" And to somebody who shushed him: "He wrote the bloody thing!" And he said to me as we watched the royal party and the cast enter the cinema: "You cunt!"

"Stop f—— about you lot or get out," somebody told us.

On the way back we stopped and ate fish and chips in the car. Albert got the piece with bones in it which made him more irritable. He had to keep spitting.

"I wonder what Somerset Maugham's doing," he said.

Diana said, "Be peaceful, petal."

It was the first time I had really looked at her. She knew this and smiled at me, sympathetically.

"He's my milkman, too!" she said. He had recruited her. It explained the beehive of scarlet hair with the white camellia in it, the two-inch ear-rings, the skin-tight white sharkskin dress with its precipitous front which missed her apparently naked nipples by a hair's-breadth and the bare feet. Her make-up I can only describe as dramatic; you felt that she wanted to take off her eyelashes to eat her chips. Her voice I would have recognised again but nothing else.

I pressed her hand.

I was a constant disappointment to Albert. After the abortive première he tried several other things. He tried to persuade me to get arrested on a drunk charge or slap somebody's face in public in order to get my name in the headlines.

"You're not a wild liver, are you," he would say, critically.

Now his tack was asking me to let him speak to people for me, make contacts, get himself a position of power in the film industry so that he could do something for me.

"*I'll* get him a distribution contract," he said that night when I told him some of Norman Freville's difficulties.

You go along with people like that because often they

[15]

express your own secret desires. I wanted to be rich and famous but I was too busy nursing my talent.

"You spend too much time pigging away at that typewriter," Albert used to say.

Work didn't come into Albert's idea of success. I should be getting big cheques, drinking with the right people in the right places, my name in all the papers, television interviews, flying to Hollywood.

"Flying to Hollywood for what?" I would say. "To sit in a room and write."

"Don't give me that," Albert would say. "You just lie back and come up with the odd idea and have a lot of long-legged nymphos taking it down."

This is the kind of dream that gets rubbed out the first time you spend the best summer for years writing the same film script nine times. Borrowing money right and left on expectation of commencement payments, delivery payments, first-day-of-shooting payments. You couldn't convey any of this to Albert. He didn't even listen.

"You should let me handle it for you," he would say.

He had the calm swinging confidence you come out of a Cary Grant film with; but Albert had it all the time.

"Look at that lovely arse," Albert said.

The bar girl was stooping with her legs straight to pick up glasses from the floor under the dart board. You could see the tops of the stockings and now her face as she smiled round at us.

"This is Horace Spurgeon Fenton, the writer," Albert told her. "He's looking for a girl to play a small part in one of his films."

"Can I have your glasses?" she asked.

I don't know which hurt me most of those two lines.

Albert caught her hand. "I'm serious, darling."

"That's what frightens me," she said.

We laughed and so did a few customers.

"You must have heard of Horace Spurgeon Fenton?" Albert said.

"I'll bet there's a good many as has!" the girl cried. And to me she said: "Will you tell your friend I regret to say I'm already under contract to Mr Palmer for the next two years an' if I break it I have to refund me fare from Ireland to him—" and with mock threat to Albert: "Unless I get married of course, then it's compassionate leave!"

It got a laugh again from everybody except Albert who had become thoughtful. "I've heard about that," he said. "Talk about the white slave traffic! Fancy getting that for two years for the price of her fare from Ireland?"

I started talking to him on the drive home but he shut me up. We were passing water on the tow-bar of his caravan when he spoke again.

"I think I'm on to something big," Albert said.

This was the beginning of the Irish thing.


Tres had shut the garage doors. I opened them to get in and left them open. I don't like shut doors. It was about one o'clock, a dark night, chilly and clear after rain. I crept round the house and trod on the hedgehog's saucer.

"Is that you dad?" Fiona's voice came from the window above.

"No, it's a burglar."

"Mum wants some money."

I went indoors, wiped my feet on the kitchen doormat, walked through the clean, polished, aerosoled house, stepping carefully over a patchwork quilt of sleeping cats.

"Have you got any money?" Fiona was sitting up squinting at me and yawning. She was about ten, cynical and hardy. She had had three eye operations and enjoyed them all. I told her that I would pawn my typewriter tomorrow.

"Oh no! Not again! Big deal!"

"You have to starve," I said.

"That depends what you want to be," she said.

Here was a child who read everything of mine; brought her friends in and went through old manuscripts and bits

I'd discarded as too hot. She knew the worst about me but it also gave us some understanding. She had been kidnapped once when she was a baby. It happened when I was at Edna's or somewhere else of course. Everything happened to Tres while I was away. Polio, bailiffs, electricity cut off, water cut off, gas stoves taken, furniture reclaimed. She had toured the town with the police and found Fiona with some mother-complexed adolescent idiot child. Tres had beaten her up in the police station.

"You should have got publicity on that," Albert said.

Nobody wise would kidnap Fiona now.

"I'll make you a cup of tea?" I liked to keep somebody awake with me.

"Don't bother."

I kissed her goodnight and went into Lewis's room in the hope of interesting him but I couldn't wake him up. I listened at Tres's door then went to my own room and organised my working-at-night tape. A recording of spasmodic typing, guitar playing, chinking cups and so on.

"This is the sort of thing that gives me fresh hope," Albert would say.

I undressed, left the recorder going, went down and out of the house in pyjamas and slippers, got the side of an old cot and placed it against Alice's window and climbed in.

"Get out!" Alice hissed.

But she couldn't do much about it without making a row and she was frightened of Tres.

She was a young schoolteacher I'd met on a train when I was working on a television series. I'd got her interested in the series and somehow managed to con Tres into letting her come and watch our set once a week. After that we conned together and she became a lodger. She was young, pretty, freckled. She wore a striped school scarf and blazer, a short gym skirt, black stockings, played hockey and tennis in divided skirts.

"Oh my gawd!" Albert used to say when she breezed past and he saw my face.

I was always looking at her.

"I want you," I told her one night when the family was in bed.

"Don't be fantastic, Fenton," she said.

I'd analysed her by that time. I'd tried everything else. I'd even taken her abroad. I knew I'd never get her interested in romance so I got her interested in contraceptives—it was the one thing I could beat her on.

"I've never seen one before," she said. She put it on her finger. She said: "I have to keep one step ahead of the class."

I had sent her to her room and established our new relationship.

I didn't find the note from Tres until three o'clock in the morning. It was stuck in my typewriter.

*Freville flying to Hollywood. Wants script with two copies his place nine o'clock latest. Cutting off telephone on Wednesday. That girl will have to go. Please leave at least five shillings for dinner—T.*

These little notes were almost our only means of communication these days. I wouldn't have found it then if the Monster had not started banging in her room and woken Alice.

I rang Freville's Ambassador number five consecutive times before getting a reply.

"For God's sake!" a girl's voice answered at last.

"Sorry it's so late. Can I speak to Mr Freville?"

"You can try, darling. I gave up hours ago. Norman!" I heard her say. "Norman! Oh, you pig!" There were the sounds of a short fight and she came back: "Who is it?"

"Horace Fenton. It's about the script—"

"Horace *Spurgeon* Fenton? How are you? I love your books. I'm Jane Chappell."

"Chappell?"

"No, atheist—" she laughed and went straight on:
"Sorry, that's always irresistible. Chappell—like the pianos?
My old man is a French count with an 'o'—*stop* it, Norman! God, he's lying on top of me. We're on the rug.
We're off to Hollywood in the morning. Why don't you
come Horace? It'd be good for your writing. Norman says
why aren't you here with that f—— script?"

There was a short scramble and then Freville's voice:
"Hello, chum—are you on the way?"

"Just leaving," I told him.

"Well for God's sake. You know what this means?"

"I didn't know you were going today."

"Nor did I. I got financial backing."

"I'm playing the Caroline part!" came the girl's voice
as if to explain it.

"I haven't promised anything, darling."

"*Now* he tells me!"

"How long will you be?"

"Are you going to see . . . ?" I mentioned an international
film star he'd been negotiating for.

"I'm going to sign him up. You may have to re-write for
him."

"I'll be there," I said.

"You'd better be, chum!"

I found my ninth re-write under a neat pile of blue summonses and judgment summonses, mortgage murmurs,
threats and notices of eviction, gas bills and desperate
SOSs from Edna and anxious letters from my grown-up
children. Signals and salutes, not birthday reminders.

I lay on the bed to skim through the script which was
still lacking the ending. There were at least three major
scenes still to write before I drove to London. Still to invent.
A dozen endings had come out of the last few script conferences, all predictable. I was glad Freville had been too
drunk to ask how I had finished it off.

I put a top foolscap and four carbons into the Olympia
and started typing.

EXT: JOAN'S STREET AND HOUSE: DAY

It was scene 284, page 140 with at least ten more pages to write. But the idea was now complete. Some things are purposely planted in a story with the object of maturing into a situation at the end; some things occur out of character or plot which only afterwards suddenly blaze with significance. Out of all the lies my leading character had told purely because he was a liar, I now saw one which could come to roost and give me a twist for the end of the picture.

At five o'clock I entered my wife's bedroom very quietly.

"Tres," I said.

She screamed.

"It's only me," I said. "Where's the stapler?"

I went out of her bedroom so that she could get out of bed unobserved. A moment later she came into my room wearing her old coat over her round shoulders and whatever she wore in bed; short, iron-grey hair had been swiftly combed and she'd got her false eyelashes on. She picked up the stapler from under my nose and banged it down.

She stomped out and down into her house while I got on with the work. I could hear and sense her in the rooms below; scooping up a half-eaten rat I'd noticed on the stairs and whatever else was going, putting it God knows where, cleaning and polishing the offending patches, going through with an aerosol spraying scent and removing any hint that cats aren't clean, putting on milk for coffee.

We didn't quarrel any more. The shouting was over. The more she found out about me the more I revolted her. I never stood a chance really with Tres. She didn't seem my generation. Nobody over thirty does. She had the high-principled, clean-cut philosophy of a cowboy and had published ten novels about them. She used to have letters from her readers starting *"Dear Buck."*

I telephoned the dairy.

"Is Albert Harris there?"

"Who? No. He doesn't work here. Is that the police?"

"Tell him it's Horace," I said.

I heard the rattling of milk churns and doors slamming. "Albert! Albert! Where's old fartarse? You're wanted mate! They're after you!"

"Horace?" came Albert's sleepy voice. "Jesus. Only just got me head down. What is it?"

I told him.

"Give me an hour," he said.

He turned up an hour later in the dairy van. He had brought me a five-gallon drum of dairy petrol to start the script on its way to Hollywood and at least two pounds' worth of dairy produce for Tres—everything from bacon through cream and butter to tinned peaches.

"You should be going to Hollywood not him," Albert said. "You know more about the story than he does."

I told him that it looked like going through at last. Once they start spending money on trips to Hollywood they have to try to get it back. There comes a point when making the picture is cheaper than not making it.


Norman Freville was lying on his back on the scarlet couch reading my latest re-write.

"This is going to choke you, mate."

The thing, these days, is to be a prole.

"Gimme the last one."

I got down the top copy from the pile of foolscap bound scripts in yellow, green, red, blue, pink, white, black and grey. They started in April and came right through the summer.

"Now the next one—green."

I gave him the green one which he also scanned.

"You know what's happened?" he said. "We've over-polished it. We've lost the original texture—your first roughage. Especially on some of the characters. Listen to this : 'Poor bloody housewives—they put up with the same thing day after day for the sake of the same thing night

[22]

after night!'" he laughed. "I like that! We've lost it. Why?"

"We lost it in June," I reminded him. "First we transferred it to Joan then you thought it was too coarse for her."

"Gimme the blue—no, the white. Tell you what, give me your first rough draft—I mean, that's what sold *me* on the story and he'll be seeing it for the first time...."

He lay there laughing and reading and cleaning out his ears. "This is marvellous. I'd forgotten what it was about. Would you believe it the first one is the best?"

"I have said that," I said.

"Well, you're absolutely right, chum, you really are."

The whole summer had been wasted. No writer has a summer to spare. It had cost me two thousand pounds, borrowed.

"We've got time to give it a new title page and a clean cover," he said.

The new title page was so as to include both our names as authors, not that film credits ever bothered me. The new cover was to keep me busy right up until the last possible moment. He was worried as hell I might write a short story while he was away. I sat at my little table in the corner while he lay on the scarlet couch and talked about the trip to Hollywood. Hardly able to keep my eyes open I retyped the title page, unstapled the staples with the point of the scissors, robbed the new script of its covers and put them on the script I had written last winter before we had the first of our thousand conferences.

"Hurry up, I think he's here!"

The managing director of the distribution company putting up a third of the production costs dependent upon the National Film Finance Corporation putting up the other two-thirds dependent upon the right star being engaged dependent upon my script came in to take Norman Freville to London Airport.

"Don't fight him, Norm!" I heard him say behind my back as I drove in the last staples.

[23]

"Don't worry, Solly."

"I know you, Norm. I'm worried. Look, if he wants his own director let him have his own director. If he wants his masseur—you know about his masseur?—we'll meet him. If he wants the story re-written. . . ."

He petered out and I could sense that Freville had drawn his attention to me working in the corner.

"Hello—there—Horace," Solly said. "I want to congratulate you—wonderful story, wonderful script. Paramount are crazy about it." (It was always Paramount.) And to Freville: "Paramount are backing his salary no-matter-what for eighty-per cent U.S. and overseas—I been talking to Hollywood. Which are your bags?"

"Do you mind?" Freville said to me as I gave him the completed script.

I picked up two heavy bags and followed them out.

"Oh God!" Freville had stopped to look back into the flat. "This bloody shambles. Bit of a party last night, Horace, you should have been here!"

"You should have invited me—"

"Look, chum, I can't let Mrs P. see this. She comes in at ten to clean up and she adores me, you know? Could you just skate round it?"

"Sure."

"Come on, come on," said Solly. And as we went down the stairs: "The one they're telling about Frankie over there—at three pounds a minute Atlantic rates, you know? There was this studio hand wanted to impress his girl friend and he goes up to Frankie and says: 'Would you do me a great personal favour? I've told my girl I know you and she's visiting today—would you come up to me and say "Hallo, Al?"' 'Sure, bud,' said Frankie. Later he sees the studio hand and his girl and he goes across. 'Hiya, Al!' he says and claps him on the back. The studio hand turns round and says, 'Why don't you f—— off?'"

They drove away laughing and forgot to say goodbye.

I gave the flat a thorough clean. It took an hour to do all

the washing-up though there was plenty of hot water. We couldn't get much hot water at home, either home. We only ran the immersion heaters when we could afford it. He had a vacuum cleaner which I enjoyed using. Things like that we'd never had. A reading lamp you could switch off when you're in bed to save getting out. A refrigerator we never had. It was nice to put ice in cold drinks.

I moved all the heavy furniture and cleaned the carpet, scrubbing the wine stains with soapy water. After that I dusted the wooden surfaces—it was a kind of cedar redwood and came up well. Then I used furniture cream on everything and polished it. I put all the records and books and magazines away. There was one of my own titles on the floor under the radiator which I suppose the Countess had seen. I found a two-shilling piece under an armchair and put it in my pocket, then worried about it and put it on the mantelpiece.

His charwoman came in. She didn't like finding me there alone. She went into the bedroom and when she came out I could see that she had something to say. I felt nervous. I've always been bullied by women.

"Have you been in the bedroom?" she said.

"Not yet," I lied. "I was going to do that next."

I could see that she didn't believe me.

"You do the typing, Mr Fenton," she said, "and I'll do the cleaning."

I had been there the whole summer and she thought I was the typist. Before I left she called me into the kitchen.

"Did you do that?" she said.

The top of the electric stove was scratched. I might have done it, I didn't know. I felt angry at being in a false position.

My fee for the whole film was to be five thousand pounds. I had been paid five hundred on starting the original treatment nearly a year ago and five hundred on delivery in the spring. Then I got five hundred on starting the draft screenplay which I was still writing and re-writing in order to get another five hundred delivery payment. If Norman succeeded in signing the star I would get the five thousand plus the first half of the remaining three thousand pounds for final script in one lump—two thousand pounds in all followed by another fifteen hundred on completion.

It was the typewriter pawning stage in other words for my borrowings had reached the top limit. I remember thinking as I watched the pawnbroker make out the ticket on the Olympia that Freville, the Countess, the script and the Stratocruiser would be getting near to the North Pole.

# 3

# Edna

ON THE SATURDAY, about the same time that Norman Freville was grumbling to the Countess about being whisked
off to a party in Beverly Hills because he had lost twelve
hours somewhere between the speed of the Stratocruiser
and the sun resulting in fatigue (I got this afterwards) I was
sitting in Hanger Lane on my way to take Edna to the
pictures.

Albert was with me. If he wanted to persuade me to do
anything he would go with me to the lavatory. He was
trying to get me to invest half of the two thousand pounds
I had got coming in his Irish thing. His idea was to start
a country club (brothel) staffed with a dozen lovely Irish
domestics (prostitutes) to cater for tired business men
(whoremongers) who would be willing to pay Albert (ponce)
five guineas an evening including the drink (stolen). The
brackets are mine.

He had got his eye on the old vicarage in my road which
was to let fully furnished for seven guineas a week on a
year's lease. The girls he could get through a domestic
agency in Dublin at twelve-pounds-ten each.

"To keep within the law they just have to do a bit of
dusting sometimes," he said. He always had the little
details to make the big things seem plausible. "They'll fall
over themselves to come. You can come with me to make a
final selection. We fly to Dublin and put up at the Royal
Oak for auditions."

I would defy anybody to find fault with it.

"It would be a steady income for you," Albert said.

There was the usual traffic jam in Hanger Lane.

I always seemed to be sitting there. It was a kind of No-Man's-Land, halfway between one battle-field and the other. I relaxed there. I used to belong to myself there.

"You'd be independent," Albert said. "You could pick and choose your pictures. You wouldn't be pushed around so much. Lapping after these bastards with your tongue hanging out."

"It's not really my two thousand, Albert." It was always all laid out.

"Rubbish man. Who earned it? You want to get it in cash. Don't even put it into the bank. That's where you go wrong."

"They give *me* money."

"Well, that's their job after all," he said.

"What about a licence?" I asked.

"I've been into that with a solicitor," Albert said. He had several customers who were solicitors. He must have brightened their lives. "I apply for a club licence. Members only."

"How do you explain the girls?"

"I don't have to explain them. They're domestics, that's the beauty of it. We just happen to be over-staffed, that's all. If a drinks licence is difficult we'll serve coffee. Nobody's going to give a damn what they drink."

"They'll have you for running a disorderly house."

"Who's going to talk? It'll be a godsend in a place like ours. Save people going up the West End all the time. Besides, the girls are all Catholics. Our town is riddled with Catholics. They're like the Jews, they hang together. Don't get the wrong idea, Horace. We're not running a rowdy house. They're not going to prance around in tights, you know. You saw Mary? They're all like that. Nice co-operative girls you give 'em twenty quid a week and a bit to send home to the old priest."

He had been to see the girl at the pub since our visit and had delicately sounded her out.

"She likes the idea," he had reported.

I wonder whether she knew the idea.


Hawthorn Way had the sad, silent, community-mourning appearance of a recent pit-head disaster. My car seemed out of place. So did Albert in his dog-tooth check. Edna followed us in from one of the muttering groups.

"They've took the chairs if you know it or not!"

She was tempering anger because of Albert's presence. She thrust the execution warrant into my hand.

"That's not even one of my debts!"

It was one of Tres's debts. If I got mixed up what chance had outsiders?

"Look at this room!" Edna said.

It looked empty without the dining-room chairs. "And they've took Lang's enlarger and projector!" she said. "He wonarf be wild when he comes in."

"We're starting a new business," Albert told her, consolingly, really fishing for support. He looked round with a pained expression. "She ought to have a better place than this, Horace. Supposing some newspaper reporter ferreted out this tatty old family? Where's your public image? I mean, when somebody's got two wives you expect one of them to be a lush piece. Who was the home-breaker? One's old and the other's even older. No offence, Mrs Fenton," he said, noticing Edna's expression, and then, as if sympathising with her. "A bloody old charwoman. Well isn't that right?" he asked her, fairly.

"What picture d'you want to see?" I asked her.

She cheered up. She was always afraid I was going to make an excuse not to go. A thing like the chairs going helped her on a Saturday. She had the picture and what time it started. The ride in the front seat of the Hurricane past the neighbours offset whatever stature she might have lost. The pictures and a choc ice made her week. Tres kept me up to it.

Albert, helping, told her about a coffee-bar in town which had orange boxes instead of chairs. "It's really the thing now. But don't paint them," he said. "It's no good if you paint them."

She was a little woman and her mouth had sunk in and I expect she had feelings tucked away somewhere but I couldn't be bothered with them any more.

"Oh, mate!" Albert said when I took him out. He looked along the street of rough-cast council houses. "How do I get out of here?"

I instructed him about buses.

"Don't forget," he said. "It wouldn't cost you five guineas as a shareholder. A free evening whenever you like."

He had struck the only incentive that mattered.


Sue came in from a dance with one of her boy friends about half-past eleven and found me sandpapering orange boxes, Edna stuck to the television. She was a compulsive viewer and you would often find her watching the blank screen during the day when there was nothing on.

"Hello, daddy darling," Sue said and to the boy: "This is daddy darling. Daddy darling this is—what was your name again?" She was a humorist. All four girls were humorists and the boy Lang was their stooge, Edna a kind of comedian's prop. "What is daddy darling doing?"

"They're chairs," Edna told her. "Bloody orange boxes." You could tell the picture was over.

"They are chic," I explained. "You wouldn't know that."

"Don't shout at her then," Sue said. "She's not stupid. You're not stupid, are you mummy? MUMMY! Okay, so she's stupid. Don't rub it in."

The pit-head disaster emerged at about three o'clock in the morning. It wasn't the chairs going but something real.

Real issues never bothered Edna. Lang had come in after his mother and sister had gone to bed and was helping me finish off the orange boxes. We were both getting enthusiastic about them now.

"We could use these little shelves as book shelves," Lang said.

"Or you could put your feet on them like bar stools," I said.

I showed him.

Lang would have been about eighteen, a year older than Sue, though his tree was shorter. I had planted a tree for each birth in the council-house garden. He was a nice comradely sort of chap and had taken the loss of his photographic equipment stoically as I knew he would. He believed in fame and fortune too and wasn't too worried about what intervened. He had fallen out of my car as a child and still carried the scars on his face but by now he had to point them out. We were talking about his evening.

"We met two nurses at the jazz club."

"Any good?"

"One of them's not bad. Hot stuff though. I never know what to do when they want to go on."

"Never be frightened."

"I don't want to get in a bloody mess."

"Mess your life up, you mean."

He laughed at what I had thought he might mean.

"Before you find out about girls find out about contraceptives."

"I couldn't mess about with all that sordid stuff."

"What about the other one?"

"Twenty. Too old for me."

"Is she pretty?"

"If she's too old for me she's too old for you, dad."

We were banging some new nails into the boxes when the next-door-neighbour rushed in covered in blood.

"What's happened?" he said.

I told him we were making some stools.

[31]

"Thank God," he said. "I thought the hospital had called about Mrs Fortin."

Mrs Fortin was his wife. The pit-head disaster issue which Edna had forgotten about before she got the length of the garden path was that Mrs Fortin had had a stroke and was in hospital critically ill. Frank Fortin had asked Edna if the hospital could ring her with any urgent message and would she give him a knock. Our knocking at three in the morning had woken him up and sent him falling down the stairs.

I made tea for all of us and Lang went to bed (like his eldest sister he was named after Eddie Lang, Blind Willie Dunn, the great jazz guitarist). I liked Frank but he didn't seem my generation any more than Tres and Edna were. He was a progress chaser in a factory and Edna had always held him up as a paragon.

"He comes home and digs the garden," she used to say.

And she could never get over how Mrs Fortin had a washing machine and everything on Frank's ten pounds a week while I was sometimes earning two hundred pounds a week and we'd got nothing.

"It must be the change of life," I told Frank. "She's too young to have a stroke."

"I don't know," he said. "You remember that funny turn she had before. That was some kind of pressure on the brain."

It wasn't, it was me.

"Housewives are on a hair trigger," Albert told me once. "I don't care who they are. The dustman's wife or the vicar's wife. They're quite content until you show them what they're missing and then—bang!"

That was the time when the vicar had had to move away and the vicarage had fallen empty and vacant. Albert was always cashing in on his old sins.

"She's been different ever since then, you know, Mr Fenton," Frank told me. "She doesn't know me sometimes."

It had been a time of struggling to write against the

shambles of napkins, dirt, shouting, crying, worming the children with matchsticks, clearing up their messes, the stink of pee-soaked furniture. There was the war, the factory, three nights a week electronic night classes. I was short of inspiration.

"Man creates nothing," my old chief engineer used to tell me. "His dreams and desires come from the blood he inherits and these are the fabric of his imaginings."

Mrs Fortin, neat and in her twenties, hanging out her washing in the back garden had been the loved and lusted-after heroine of dozens of my rejected stories at the time of the little back room before I met Tres. I knew her face and hair and figure, her legs, breast, every pair of panties she had and how many bras and each nightgown I knew intimately. Watching her across the typewriter through the window she kept me at heat when I needed heat. One day our eyes met and she found out about it.

I got back from work to find Edna puzzled but only mildly so.

"Mrs Fortin's upstairs in your bed," she said. "I can't get any sense out of her."

I went up and Mrs Fortin smiled at me from the pillow. A peaceful, tranquil smile, as if she'd come home.

"Are you all right?" I asked her.

"Yes, thank you," she said.

Out of her housekeeping money she had bought me a brand new copy of Bernard Shaw's *Everybody's Political What's What*. George Bernard Shaw had just died, locally. Afterwards Frank, the paragon, took it back. That's how he made his money go round.

First we got Frank in to talk to her and then he got the doctor who brought the vicar.

"She had a visitation in church last Sunday," the vicar explained to me.

"I didn't know she went to church?"

"She doesn't," Frank said. "That's the funny thing. She went last Sunday when I sent her out for the beer. She

[33]

fainted and they had to take her outside. I didn't know anything about it until the vicar just told me."

"It's quite usual with visitations," the vicar explained. "There was nothing alarming about it."

"She said something about you," Frank told me. "Didn't she, vicar?"

"Are you Mr Fenton?" the vicar said. "She thought you were Christ."

"I thought I was for a time," Albert said when I recounted this anecdote years later. "It turned out to be overwork." He was full of funny sick jokes. He would drape his arms like Christ on the Cross and say: "What a way to spend Easter?" And he used to say: "He only did it for the publicity, you know."

Mrs Fortin had gone into a mental hospital for a few weeks and when she came out she was different. I think she was better. I used to watch her pushing her roughneck boy on the garden swing and she did it as if she wanted to get rid of him. After Frank had sent the boy into the Navy he got a dog and doted on it. It was as if he'd grown potatoes to clear the ground and now he'd got the real crop.

"I'll tell you something about that dog," he was always saying.

He never told anybody anything about the boy and I never heard of him again. His wife always used to smile at me as though she was grateful for something. And now she was dying.

When the call eventually came (we had either both telephones on or nothing) I went up to tell Edna that I was taking Frank to the hospital. I couldn't wake her. I was always trying to wake people. She lay high on the pillow in a transparent black nightdress, her mouth open, her ear smelling. One of her ears had a punctured drum and the smell that came with the discharge used to mingle with the scent she used to disguise it with appalling results.

"I don't know what the old boy would do if anything

[34]

happens to Mrs Fortin," Frank said as I drove him along one of my roads. He was talking about the dog.

I asked him what her first name was. He had to think about it.

"Grace," he said at last.


Albert used to cross-examine me about my Saturday allegiance to Edna.

"I owe it to them," I said.

"You don't owe it to them," he said. "Old Tres owes it to them. She makes you go. I've heard her. You're working off her conscience, mate." He was always partly right.

I told him what Lang had told me once. That he used to cry for me at nights. Edna was like having no parents.

"He used to think his fingers were growing long. He used to lie in bed at night watching them."

Albert said: "I used to think my fingers were growing fat and they were. Look at them. Then you wonder I can't play your guitar."

Albert Harris's fingers were twice the thickness of mine. I have never mentioned it except jokingly until now but they were like deformities.

"They are deformities," he told me. "All my organs, lungs, heart, liver, kidneys, penis—twice the size of yours. If the process hadn't stopped when I was eleven I'd be dead now. I'm not supposed to drink or smoke."

"I didn't know that, Albert."

"Why do you think I'm in such a bloody hurry?" he said.

It explained why he was terrified of making a girl pregnant, of passing it on; of marriage. He just wanted to make money for his mother before he died just as I wanted to make money for my families before I lived. He was in his twenties and I was in my forties but my expectation of life was longer than his therefore I was the younger.

"Give 'em all up and marry money, mate," he told me.

[35]

"You could do more for them. They'd be better off without all this coming and going."

"Marry who? She'd have to settle all my debts. She'd have to give Tres and Edna a good payoff."

"She'd have to be shit rich," Albert agreed.

# 4

# Tres

I WENT TO SPAIN.

The international star had been signed to the picture at one hundred thousand pounds not dollars. There was a photograph of Norman Freville at London Airport ⌐ ⌐ his return from Hollywood in the London evenings.

"Why doesn't he mention you?" Albert said, when he called to see if I'd seen it. "It's your story! You should get a hundred thousand pounds."

When Freville telephoned me my line was temporarily disconnected and I got an accusing telegram:

*Your phone off please ring urgent Freville.*

It would have been *Norman* before he got the deal. "Now look, chum, and don't let me down, I want a first-rate ten-page synopsis in six copies and I want it here by four o'clock this afternoon and not five past. Now I've got . . . (he used a teeny diminutive of the star's nickname) I'm going after the top marquee names for support. It means re-angling some of those parts—we can't give them all scripts so make it good and don't be l-a-t-e!"

"I can't do it."

"What!"

"I haven't got a typewriter. It's in pawn."

"Well for God's sake get it out!"

"I haven't got any money."

"How much is it?"

"Ten pounds."

"Ten pounds! Do you realise I've got a three-hundred-thousand-pound movie on my hands, pal?" The weekend in California had Americanised him.

After the ninth re-write and the whole of the summer gone and in hock for more than I could earn on the rest of this picture and my problematical next job I was given the five hundred delivery payment quickly as a great favour. My agent stopped two hundred I owed him plus his fifty commission and I gave the two-fifty balance to everybody in my capacity as financial middleman.

There was just enough left for two weeks housekeeping, petrol and cigarettes.

Spain was a bonus.

"He can't work in this country because of his tax position. In fact he would be arrested as soon as he stepped off the plane. We're going to shoot it in Spain. It means a little re-angling, of course."

"It's supposed to be the Home Counties!"

"Well that's why I'm taking you with us to look for locations. It'll give you a full week to get the locale and idiom."

The only locale and idiom a writer has is in his bones.

"Incidentally he wanted to use his own writer—you know about his writer? I wouldn't hear of it," Freville said.

There was soon a day when I drove into the car-park at London airport, locked up the car and wandered away carrying Lang's holdall which I'd bought him for twenty-five shillings to go to Austria with his school. It still bore some of the labels. I hoped it made me look a little more international than I felt. Freville and the beginnings of the film unit were at a bar inside the building.

"This is Horace Spurgeon Fenton, the author," he said, quickly, to counteract the impression I might have created. "So you managed to get away from homes?"

He used the plural as a joke and everybody laughed as

he explained it. He was inclined to retail my confidences in company and although sometimes I felt sick at betraying people who mattered to me sometimes again I was glad that perhaps the company might find me amusing or likable.

"This is the author who has never seen one stage play in his life—tell them Horace."

"I've never seen one stage play in my life."

He always got a bigger laugh than I did.

"I couldn't fix you in at the Hilton, Horry old chap," he told me as we went to the plane. "I've got you booked at the San Francisco—it's just a little ways up the Avenida Jose Antonio. The Gran Calle."

He was going from a Spanish lilt to an American accent with lots of "shit man!" and he was wearing dark glasses.

"You'll be more comfortable there," he said looking at my holdall. "It's very homely."

I was terrified. I had only been abroad once before and that was with Alice the schoolteacher in charge. I managed to get her away for an expensive week during the early seduction period and she had taken care of me as though I were the infant class, getting me across roads, speaking French to the waitresses for me.

"For God's sake, Fenton! Don't call waitresses 'darling' over here. You'll get a knife in your back!"

She kept giving me Russian tea and escargots because she didn't want to appear bigoted and I couldn't change the bloody order. In the grounds around the Eiffel Tower (she was angry because I daren't go up in the lift) I picked her a piece of lilac and got the police on to me.

"I thought you'd do something like this!" she snapped almost in tears as he rattled on at me about the regulatons.

The gendarme's only bewilderment was why I had picked it for *her*. Then she slipped in the bathroom of the Paris hotel—she had chosen a cheap place in the Rue Blanche— and the tap, a tall spiked waterworks, went right up her arse. The next morning because of her pronunciation she took me to the wrong station and bought two tickets to

Caen in Normandy instead of Cannes on the Riviera. We had a wet cold week on the English Channel which we could have got for a tenth the price and trouble in Brighton. By the time we got back the romance had slipped and that's when I had stated my terms.

Madrid was better. I fell in love with a very pretty American girl called Lois from Buffalo. What seldom happens to me is that she was in the next bedroom at the San Francisco hotel. I drank enough to get the courage to knock her door and ask if she had any toothpaste.

"I wondered how you would do it," she said.

It was one of those nice, easy, funny relationships with a stranger without strain and purely platonic.

"I'm going to hold your hands all night," she said when we were in bed together.

I only ever raped one woman and although I didn't know it she was unconscious. I thought she was sulking. This is a significant bit of the future and not the kind of important event you could expect from your horoscope.

There is a novel in the making of a picture which I will never write for to me films are as important as tinsel is to Christmas. I avoided the film crowd while I was in Madrid and they didn't seem to need me. I got glimpses of them hanging around the Puerto del Sol and again at the Prado museum; rain-coated, sports-jacketed, mooching around in bored groups, Norman Freville in his film director's sheepskin coat never mind the temperature panning the possible shots with his hands held up like a view-finder.

The girl with him was different. Film people fall roughly into two classes; the unglamorous technicians and the glamorous artistes. The girl was the Countess though I didn't realise it then; nor had I when Norman introduced me at the airport. He had missed her out with an "and you two know each other" line which you always got with the one person you don't know and would maybe like to. What he had in his mind I expect was that we had met on the telephone the night before the Hollywood trip. She hadn't spoken to me this time but I sensed that she was watching me. I didn't actually look at her except sideways. Glamorous people intimidate me in some peculiar chemical way. Especially film actors and actresses with their studio-issue teeth and sun-lamp complexions. There is more uniformity at the top of the ladder than you ever meet at the bottom. Maybe I'm just ugly and I'm jealous.

"Your teeth look as though somebody's dynamited a graveyard," Tres once told me. A non-western writer would have said "bombed".

Anyway, I stayed with Lois the whole time. We kept each other laughing—mostly about my troubles. I had the habit of throwing out lifelines to strangers (to rescue me) and although I often only came up with an old boot sometimes I got genuine interest and this I have always been able to return. I solved a lot of her family problems—whether her brother should marry a girl from Cincinatti, if her mother's asthma would benefit from a sea climate (it wouldn't) and what their attitude should be about socialised medicine.

I have never been to America but when you know it from people like Saroyan, Frank Harris, Bing Crosby, Thurber, Steinbeck, Hemingway, Scott Fitzgerald, Robert Nathan, Truman Capote, Eddie Lang, Joe Venuti, Bix Beiderbecke, Muggsy Spanier, Miff Mole, Marilyn Monroe, there is no need to go there. Tres and I had both had books published in the States which were set in the States and nobody ever questioned their authenticity even though neither of us had been farther west than High Wycombe. I would say it is better if you have not been there. Some English writers have a better American literary accent than some American writers. This is partly because culturally the Americans have exported everything down to their fingernails.

Lois and I used to sit in the American Bar of the San Francisco hotel on the Avenida Jose Antonio and I used to tell her about the origins of Storyville in the French Quarter of New Orleans, Telegraph Hill and the Golden Gate in 'Frisco, the old Savoy Ballroom in Harlem, New

York, the old fellow who used to send Saroyan out for buns from the Eastern Telegraph office in Fresno and the day the dam broke in Columbia.

"Haven't you ever sailed on Chesapeake Bay?" I asked her.

"Where?" she said.

Lois told me about Buffalo and vacations at lakeside cottages; about boy friends and broken engagements and how serious she felt about marriage and sex and religion. I got to know her family by their first names and the streets of Buffalo by their numbers and names; the rivers and mountains of America I got to know again and the terminology attaching to American life, schooling, work, transport, shops, clothes, travel, morals, necking, philosophy, history, her work in the Real Estate office and wet nights reading in her front room.

"*Que est dos Espagna?*" Freville asked me on the rare occasions we met.

"Swell," I said.

Lois and I went shopping together in the big Madrid departmental stores for presents for my families and hers. She let me buy her a keepsake brooch and she bought me a black fighting bull with its head down, charging, and coloured banderillas sticking out of its neck. We visited a bullfight and pretended to be horrified and we took a trip out to a bull ranch, to Toledo to see El Greco's studio, to a public dance in the *Plaza Mayor* very late at night. We drank and ate in innumerable cafés and in seven days became inseparable.

"Do you mind if I get a hair-do?" she would ask.

"I'm just going to the lavatory," I would say.

We waited for each other. I get families quickly.

One night at the end the bedroom door opened and a *Guardia* came in with the lift boy who had informed on us.

"It is illegal, senor."

"What is illegal?"

"It is illegal for a man and woman in a hotel bedroom."

"We're not doing anything!"

"I just wish we had been," Lois said. "It's outrageous."

They stayed by the door while we got out of bed and the *Guardia* escorted me back to my room. We were both as deeply hurt as if we had been long married and now torn asunder.

To part, because she was wearing shorts which were illegal, we had to go miles out of the town into the woods, and then come all the way back again.


"I hope you've made plenty of notes," Freville said as we flew back.

The girl with him, who I still didn't know was the Countess, was watching me again as though she knew I hadn't been making notes. An improvement I noticed about her however this time, flying back from Madrid, was that her back teeth, compared with the ones in the window, were slightly yellow as if she didn't take that much trouble. I liked her a little more and almost met her eyes once or twice.

When I got back from Spain Alice had gone and her room had been redecorated and fumigated.

"I got rid of her," Tres said.

She was taking off her gardening gloves as though she'd done it with a spade.

"I couldn't stand it any longer," she said. *"Nymphs and Shepherds* every night on that damned tin whistle!"

Alice had to keep one step ahead of her class in everything. In sex I doubt whether she made it.

"I like the wallpaper," I told Tres. I was always sucking up to her to try to lighten the atmosphere. It was like saying "I like your hair." Tres bought wallpaper the way other women buy clothes.

"The paintwork needed an undercoat," she said.

This was to tell me that the last of her housekeeping money had gone on wallpaper. She didn't like decorating

[43]

any more than she liked cooking, housework or gardening —or children for that matter—but everything had to be right. You weren't allowed to set fire to a bit of steak and get it crisp on the outside and raw in the middle because that would splash the stove. In the garden she would have done away with Autumn altogether—the ruck and storm-drift and dead leaves of Autumn were as untidy as the life I led and just as much an irritation to her.

She had other qualities though. She was intrepid. One night she climbed a railway shunting-yard fence to steal coal for the fire because we had a film producer coming and we had to keep up some kind of front. And it didn't take much to cheer her up. When the bailiff turned up on his Quickly with a judgment summons he had to give me two shillings and ninepence as my fare to court.

"Something always turns up," she used to say.

She varied, really, but always on the side of gloom. Albert called her Lorna Doone. She was always running away and the children and I were always fetching her back. She didn't have much imagination when it came to hiding out. She loved to sit in a tea shop because she didn't have to do the washing up. She had about four favourite towns and tea shops. I'd like as many pounds as I've pegged out the car in a side-turning with Lewis and Fiona, watching tea-shop entrances. We shared the certainty that we were never going to see her again and our hearts used to come up every time we saw a pair of stooped shoulders and a straw hat.

"No wonder we're mixed up," my daughter Fiona used to say.

They had a sense of humour that kept them from crying. They had reason to know that she was capable of suicide.

"Have you promised Albert anything?" Tres asked me now. "He keeps waking me up to see if there's any news."

Albert used to drop the empties if he wanted attention in the early mornings. I told her I hadn't promised him anything though I didn't know what he'd promised himself.

[44]

"His mother's been round to see me," Tres said. "Don't get him mixed up with any of your bad-hats."

London was the badlands and anybody I knew there was an outlaw. I gave her the Spanish fighting bull that Lois had helped me to choose. She accepted it but she was also disgusted. Had I been to a bullfight? Yes, I had, hadn't I. She might have known.

"You're more sentimental about meat than you are about animals," she said.

I distributed Spanish coins to all the children in both homes and a few days later I was collecting them back to change at the bank. They had kept them for me. Over those years I was averaging about nine thousand pounds a year and nobody had more than one pair of shoes.

The bank manager called me in that week. Not by telephone or letter but by bouncing a dozen of the small cheques I had written when I paid in the balance of the five hundred delivery payment before going to Spain.

"Sorry about that," he said, "but it's the only way I can attract your attention."

"You shouldn't have bounced the Court one," I told him. "It'll get the bailiff into trouble."

"We can't afford to have favourites," he said.

I told him there was fifteen hundred pounds due in next Tuesday, anticipating that the picture was now going through and making the date firm for his sake.

"There always is," he said. And he said: "It's these films that seem to cost you so much money. Whenever you say you've got another five thousand pounds contract I know we're in for a bad spell. Couldn't you stick to books?"

I get a bit offended when people think they know what's best for me. I explained that I was too heavily committed now. It was a fortune or nothing. Books didn't make enough money.

"But Compton MacKenzie's got an island. A whole island."

"He's a best-seller. One best-seller and you're away."

[45]

"But surely that football story was a best-seller? It was in all the papers. That's what put you on television. You couldn't have a bigger success than that?"

"Actually sales weren't very high though it was a literary success," I told him.

It was not my book. We had this permanent misunderstanding that you get with some people. There was another writer named Fenton, Charles Fenton, who had written a best-seller about a footballer. There was a film which had also been an artistic success. I met the other Fenton once at a party at Brown's Hotel given by our American publishers—I was in their thriller list. He was being lionised; so young, too, straight out of a provincial university and trying hard to suffer and starve in the short time before he cashed in. I knew he would never do it.

I got the bank manager to raise me another twenty-five pounds and took five in my pocket. It always seemed like a fortune.

He was right about pictures, though.

"Norman Freville wants me to write a picture for him," I had told Tres at the beginning of that year.

Afterwards her psychiatrist told me never to tell her anything that might set her back.

# 5

# The Countess

ALBERT HAD BEEN CHAFING all this time and now he came round with a selection of glossy pictures of Irish girls.

"Aren't they going to think it peculiar your asking for pictures of domestic servants?" I asked him.

"They don't give a damn whether it's peculiar or not," he said. "All they give a damn about is getting hungry mouths out of the country and getting money in. Ireland exports people the way other countries export products. When do you get the fifteen hundred? It hasn't fallen through, has it? I've committed myself."

I told him that Freville was probably waiting for the American deal to be signed covering the star's salary.

"Why don't you ring him up?"

I didn't want to do any more work until he'd got the go-ahead for final script. To tell the truth I didn't want to see that bloody script again at all.

Albert picked up the receiver from my desk (we were on again). "Let me telephone Paramount and find out what they're up to? How do you ring New York?"

I put the phone down again. I told him that we were going to have a night out on my five pounds. This was a very rare occasion for me, to go to London to a club or somewhere, do something civilised, to live like a novelist and scriptwriter.

"Can I bring Harold?" Albert asked.

Harold was an embossed wallpaper inventor Albert was cultivating. He never had all his eggs in one basket.


I met the Countess again and again I failed to know who she was. This was the third or fourth or fifth time, counting our brushes in Madrid. Up until then I discovered later, she had been wooing Freville for what she wanted; but tonight a balloon of some kind had gone up between them and after that until the day he shot her he was wooing her. It was all to do with money and power and not love. I never came across straightforward love in Wardour Street, the street of illusions. It was too simple. Nothing to do with morals. Love is too simple for them, except on the screen. Anything smaller than a package deal and they don't want to know.

Freville came into the club escorting the girl who was dressed and made up like something. Where I would have been sitting on my own, Albert had taken us across to join some well-known faces in a dining alcove. One was a star Australian singer whom Albert greeted like an old friend. Albert had never been to the club before. He had cracked a joke with him, showed him a card trick and told him a story all in the process of gatecrashing the table.

"We do business together," Albert explained to me in an aside. He was his milkman.

"Let me introduce the Countess," Norman Freville said as he came to the table. "She can't speak a word of English so you can say what you like—she's marvellous in bed. Aren't you, cherie?"

"Pliss?" said the girl.

I still didn't know her. I've got a blind spot on externals. I've got to know somebody really well to recognise them again. I don't look at people half the time, I think it must be. I've chatted private and confidential business to complete strangers I've met in the street and mistaken for my bank manager or accountant or even once, my brother.

I'm not short-sighted. My eyesight is good. Except old Angie—I've always known her anywhere just from the swing of her skirt.

"If you don't know them," Tres's psychiatrist told me when I mentioned this, "It means they are not fundamentally important to you."

All I can say is if this is true then of all the millions of people I've accumulated that leaves just me and old Angie.

"She thinks I asked her to have a piss," Normal Freville said after the girl had said "Pliss?"—and smiling pleasantly round the table: "Shake hands with her everybody, but don't touch her tits, they're mine."

It is the kind of crude game that some show-business people are addicted to at a certain stage of the evening in a certain environment. Everybody thinks it is hugely funny. To put it over properly you must be educated, sophisticated and capable, as everybody present must know, of kind, courteous behaviour. Preferably, you must be adored.

When everybody has committed himself with equally crude rejoinders the girl explodes the trick by asking for a drink in a Kensington accent. It is supposed to make for a good deal of embarrassment all round though the fact that the girl has been a party to it you would think would prevent this. There was a well-known actor who said "Come and sit on this, darling," and the Australian singer who had recently topped the Palladium who shook her hand, kissed it, meanwhile asking Freville which kind of venereal disease she had got and wiping his mouth on a napkin.

"You knew it was me, Horace!" the Countess Jane Chappell told me after they had joined us in the cubicle and we were all waiting for the next witty entrance.

"How should I know?" I said.

"I spoke to you on the telephone."

"Did you?" Just in time I recognised her teeth. "Madrid!" I said.

She was still smiling but getting irritated. "The night before we flew to Hollywood."

"Oh my goodness I'm sorry, of course, I do remember."

"I'm sure you do," she said, sweetly. "I must have made quite an impression. And I did say I love your books."

"Yes, you did, I know you did, that's what I remembered and in fact—"

"All right, Horace, very nice Horace, now shut up," Freville said. "This is Horace," he said to the singer.

"Horace Spurgeon Fenton, the author," the Countess said, giving Freville a kind of overriding glance. She gave them all a list of my books and films.

"You missed one out," Albert said.

"Have you got your typewriter out of pawn, Horace?" Norman Freville had listened impatiently to my build-up and now he capped it with the mark of his authority over me.

"You are a shit, Norman," the Countess said. "Why do you always try to diminish people?"

Everybody laughed as everybody does.

"I'll tell you why," the Countess went on on my behalf, "it's because like all independent film producers you're so dependent it isn't true—on writers like Horace."

"Shut your great steaming gob or tell me what I can choke you with," said Norman Freville.

He ordered drinks and the light conversation went on for it was obvious that Freville and the Countess had come in on the tail end of a blazing row.

"I ought to go now," Harold said.

Harold was a dough-faced, speckled youth of seventeen with long hair and wearing a zip-fronted motor-bike coat. Had it been leather and not plastic it would have been out of place here. We had had to get his mother's permission to bring him to London. He was drinking lager and lime.

"It's a chance to impress him," Albert had said.

Saying he ought to go was Harold's first remark since his scarlet paralysis at the earlier conversation.

"We're starting this embossed brick wallpaper company," Albert explained to the actor on his right. "Harold is in charge of the technical side."

[50]

"Good idea," the actor said, and his eyes across the table to Freville, said "Help!" but comically.

Freville said: "If you can spare the time, Horace, I'd like to get that Spanish synopsis under way tonight. We start casting on Monday."

"I have to get the boys home," I told him.

"And you have to get me home," the Countess told Freville. "And it's eleven o'clock and you can't expect leading novelists to upset their evening and go to work after midnight."

"Okay! Okay!" Freville said. "Let it pass. It's only a three-hundred-thousand-pounds movie for God's sake."

I could tell that however well-intentioned, the Countess was not doing me any good with Norman Freville.

"I tell you what we do," Albert said. This was a special treat I set out to give him on the understanding he did nothing to embarrass me. He liked the sound of his opening and the fact that he had riveted attention as one would if one interjected from the Strangers' Gallery in the House of Commons. "What we do is this. I'll take the broad home, Harold can sit in the back, maybe—then I'll meet up with you at Norm's place. Okay?"

There was a short silence. I broke it, over-anxious about Freville's expression.

"I'll go across to your place and wait outside until you get back."

"You will not," the Countess said. "You will take me home, Horace." And to Freville: "I want Horace to take me home. I want to talk about his books."

"Oh, my God," Freville said. "Do we have to make a three-act drama out of a script conference?"

"I don't mind waiting outside your place, Norman, until—"

The Countess grabbed my arm and stood up: "You will take me home—Norman, you take Horace's friends to your place for a drink. Come along, Horace."

As she led me out it occurred to me that she was using me to make him jealous.

"I really ought to go now," the wallpaper inventor was saying as we went out.

I dared not look back.

I took her (she took me) to a very lush flat in Shepherd's Market. Driving her from Shaftesbury Avenue to Mayfair in the Hurricane I gave her the full celebrity treatment; crashing gears, kerbing, wrong-turnings and sudden stops and starts.

Disconcertingly she sat with her back against the passenger door and her legs up on the seat and apart, her arms folded, watching me: observing me.

"Are you nervous, Horace?" she asked me, as we took the same one-way street for the second time round.

"Terrified. I've never driven a Countess before."

"The word is Adventuress," she corrected. "I was born in Barnstaple. My mother was half English and half Cornish. I am illegitimate. My father was an escaping prisoner from Dartmoor. I won a beauty contest at Weston-super-Mare and used the prize money to go to Rome and try to break into films. I had one or two small parts and one reasonable one and then married a French crowd artiste who happened to be a Count. He got killed doing a water-skiing stunt which was not really his job and the film company paid me ten thousand pounds' worth of lira compensation. I invested it in Swiss francs and made another three thousand pounds then came home and invested in a cosmetics business which is paying me five thousand a year on my capital. I am now trying to buy my way back into a film part. Call me Jane."

"Close your knees, Jane," I said.

She sat round in the seat, primly. "I made up the bit about the escaping prisoner."

"You've never read my books. You saw them at Norman's

[52]

place that night. They were still out when I got there."

"I've read one of them. I saw the Alcock picture and then I read the book. He used everything except the binding. It was good."

"Thank you."

"Why do you keep such low company?" she said.

"They're chums. They're from my home town."

"I mean Freville," she said.

I braked to avoid a mail van. Jane shot forward then back and the seat collapsed putting her horizontal. It was one of Albert's bird-trap's—like the "PRESS" stickers on the windscreen. She laughed up at me.

"So I misjudged you!"

"It's the first time it's ever worked."

It was the second time. The first time it lay Tres flat on her back cuddling her shopping basket. She cried because she thought it was her weight and she doesn't cry easily.

"I doubt whether you could do it like this," Jane said. And she started making the movements, experimentally.

"Keep driving," I told myself.

We came out of a back mews in Berkeley Square, went round the gardens and crabbed down to Curzon Street and the market.

"I also lied about my husband being a Count, the film parts in Rome and the ten thousand pounds," she said.

It was a good class, top-drawer prostitute's flat.


"I don't know who did this to you," she said at one stage, "but it would take me some time to put it right."

I was prepared to persevere if she would. With the pleasure I had the fascination you get from being told that you have something unusual wrong with you.

"Now," Jane said.

We did it again, beautifully.

"You see?" she said.

"What about you?" I said.

"Three times," she said. "You worry too much about other people."

The telephone had rung twice and we had ignored it. The third time she left it off the hook.

"God, that's marvellous," I said. "I've never done that before."

"Sssh!" she said.

She replaced the receiver. I was too relaxed to care. I didn't know who it was. I didn't know he had a gun. That two hours with the Countess made a nonsense of my experience, my life, Alice's "Clots" and struggling with old Angie's jodhpurs.

"You must come to Rome," Jane murmured when she saw me out and she gave my genitals a farewell pat as we kissed at the door. "I want to teach you how to kiss."

I don't know what she saw in me but whatever it was she wanted it. I think I arouse a dormant missionary instinct in some people.

When I got back to Freville's flat in Bayswater it was two a.m. Albert had been waiting outside for an hour and a half. He got into the car.

"Christ, mate! Put your heater on."

"Didn't he give you a drink?"

"He kicked us out after twenty minutes."

"You'd better wait here while I go up."

"Are you kidding? He's going to shoot you."

"Not till the final script's finished."

"He doesn't want to see you tonight—he said so. He's flaming. Did you know he's got a gun?"

I looked at Albert.

"He took it out and cleaned it."

"It's a prop."

"Famous last words. I'd stay clear if I were you, Horace. He's got something on with that pro."

"What pro?"

"The one he was with. The one you just took home."

"What makes you think she's a pro?"

[54]

"Do me a favour. I don't think, I know. Anybody would know except you. Don't tell me he's not running her. He's afraid of losing her. She's got him nervous. I expect that's where his film money's coming from. You stay out of it."

"It's nothing like that," I said.

"You didn't lay it, did you?"

I don't talk about things like that, even to Albert. Not immediately, anyway.

"You did, didn't you?"

"Where's Harold?"

"He got scared—he's hitch-hiking. We may pick him up. I told him we'd drive up the Edgware Road to Stanmore and then along the A41 to Apex Corner then up the A1."

"Has he got any money?"

"Has anybody?"

I drove north.

"What sort of gun?" I said.

"Mind you," Albert said, "It would be first-rate publicity."

He meant if I got shot.


We stood together passing water on the tow-bar of Albert's caravan when the light went up and his mother looked out.

"Albert?"

"Okay mum, nearly finished."

"Have you been with Horace Fenton? I've had the police here again! Three times! What his poor wife must go through!"

We showed ourselves in the light from the door.

"Oh, there you are," Albert's mother said to me. She liked me, she often said, but she thought I was a bad influence on Albert. She was terrified that he was shaping his life on mine. "Where's Harold Callendar?" she asked.

We told her.

"Oh, my God!" she said.

We went inside to explain the urgent film business, the script conference that had blown up.

"Anyway, I think I've got a part, mum," Albert said. "They start casting on Monday, don't they, Horace?"

"Yes," I said.

For me his ambitions were financial, for his mother apparently they were theatrical.

"Norman wants me to audition—that's the producer," Albert told his mother.

"You're not taking another day off work, are you?"

"Oh no. I explained that to him. He was very understanding. He's arranging a special camera test for me—Monday evening."

"I'd better help look for Harold," I said.

Albert said: "You can't do more than the police."

"His parents have been up here twice since midnight," Albert's mother said. "And round to yours, Horace."

"Oh God, did they get Tres out of bed?"

"Mrs Callendar said she screamed at them. Frightened them to death."

"She's a bit nervy at night," I said.

Albert said: "I'd rather be Harold than you mate."

"I do hope he's all right," Albert's mother said.

"He's all right," Albert said. "I think he enjoyed himself, don't you, Horace?"

"She's never going to let him see you again," his mother told him. "She's changing her milkman."

"Bang goes my wallpaper company," Albert said. "Oh, that reminds me," he said to me, "Freville wants the Spanish background synopsis for the casting first thing in the morning. We're having a fortnight's location shooting in Spain," he added to his mother.

It was *now* first thing in the morning. America I might have managed, but Spain was still in the public library and they didn't open until ten.

And I was more tired than usual.

# 6

# Diana

I telephoned Norman Freville at noon and he sounded normal.

"Did you get my message?" he said.

"What message?"

He wanted me to lunch in Chelsea with him and a big marquee name who was in line for the main supporting role now that we had a star to talk about. This actor was one of "The Royalty" of the profession as Norman called them. Well-known, clean-living actors and actresses who were inclined to get knighted and damed if they could just cover everything up long enough.

"Just a minute," I said.

Tres was out to the vets with one of the cats and she had forgotten even to leave a note in the typewriter.

"Well, have you finished it?" he asked.

"Yes," I said.

I hadn't done anything. What was done Old Angie had done for me at the library.

"You be here at half-past two sharp," Norman Freville said. "I'll be briefing him about the part. I'm taking him to La Caprice."

This meant that if he wasn't lumbered with me he could go somewhere halfway decent.

"What part is he playing?" I asked.

"George Atkins. He'll be marvellous. He's a real sweetie if you direct him."

I remembered Norman telling me that he had been the one to give this particular actor his little self-conscious laugh which had got him parts and made him famous.

"He's only half George's age," I pointed out.

"I'm casting against the part, naturally," he said, as though talking to an imbecile.

As fast as I created parts all through that lovely summer he was casting against them and I was re-writing.

"What's his Spanish name?" he asked.

"Pedro Gonzales Paella," I said, consulting Angie's notes.

"Isn't that a food? That's a dish!"

"Pedro Gonzales. He runs a paella bar on the Toledo road."

"That's good. What does the adaptation do to Smiley Roberts? We can't have any Bingo halls now."

"He sells lottery tickets in the Plaza Mayor."

"Wonderful. Or is that going to get us into trouble? I tell you what." I heard him clicking his fingers. "His father is a war hero. A *Franco* war hero—we gotta think about our visas. Okay?"

"Okay," I said.

"Don't be l-a-t-e," he said.

I sat looking at the clock, the typewriter, the blank sheet of paper, old Angie's sweet little librarian's notes.

Tres came in with the cat and bottles of medicine. She gave me the only urgent message she could remember. Edna was a priority concern with her and her gas stove was about to be taken again.

"If you're going gadding out again write a post-dated cheque for two pounds and tell them somebody's ill there. I'll put in that old medical certificate of mine."

She had no regard for the rules of the club. On the children's birth registrations she had filled in the date of our marriage, the town, the name of the church, all out of her head.

I sat quietly for so long trying to get the spark that she thought I'd gone.

"Say 'Mummy'," I heard her saying.

She was in the Monster's room. I bashed the typewriter to let her know I was there, I heard her go down. I felt choked. The writing started to come.

"Under titles Pilar is galloping across the hills towards the distant roofs of Valladolid, uncaring that she is endangering the life of the child within her womb."

In the original she arrived at the Bingo Hall in a taxi looking for Smiley and with the child in her arms. Everything would have to be converted from Home Counties vernacular and the characters would all talk like Arturo Conti who was the only Latin I knew. And he was Italian. In a synopsis you only needed indicative lines which was something; I only had indicative time. If I started out *now* I'd be late.

"I like *mar*nee," I said, trying to get the lilt. This is the line from *The Treasure of the Sierra Madre* just before the brigand and his pal murder the lonely traveller on his donkey if you remember. "I like *marnee*. . . ."

The film story synopsis should take its place as an art form along with other highly-polished, professional con-tricks.


"This is most extremely good, Mr Fenton," said the big marquee name who was going to be Pedro Gonzales. "I take it you have lived in Spain?"

"For a time," I said, in tune with "I like *mar*nee."

"Horace and I spent some months in the *High Sierras*. It is several *kilometros* from *Madrid*," guess-who lisped.

"Is-a very good," said the clean-cut actor, already auditioning. "What I most admire, Mr Fenton, is how you have compromised with your original conception of the story. Philosophically and dramatically. And still kept its essential truth. That is sheer professionalism."

It was sheer because I didn't give a damn. And anyway he had rehearsed that before he saw my five pages of synopsis.

When the actor had gone Norman Freville got on his couch and closed his eyes. "Now you've really got to pull up your *zapatos*," he said.

Whoever heard of anybody pulling up their shoes? His secretary who was a part-timer looked at me but I daren't meet her eyes. I didn't know until that day whose side she was on.

"The first thing is," Norman Freville said, "I want you to go right through the script and pull up his part twice as big as it's going to be. When he's signed you can cut it down again."

This was normal procedure.

"I suggest you give him the 'Same thing night after night' line for now. Translate it into the Catalan idiom of course."

We both knew it was all going to be the Wardour Street idiom.

"There's no reason why you shouldn't have a go at that now," he said. He got edgy if I wasn't doing something physical.

I got in the corner on my typewriter and did some rows of "X"s. What I had done in synopsis I now had to do in one-hundred-and-fifty foolscap pages of script. Everything from baked beans to maternity homes in the Catalan idiom. This didn't finish me. What finished me was what he said next.

"While I'm shooting this," Norman Freville said, "I want you to get on with another picture for me. I've got a three-picture deal pending with Solly."

The flat closed in on me and I couldn't breathe. I used my asthma inhaler but it didn't do anything.

"He plays that and the guitar," Freville would say to visiting celebrities when I was blowing the drug into my lungs.

"Hold up, Mr Fenton," I heard Freville's secretary say. "I think he's fainted."

"It's all these bloody late nights," I heard Freville say.

"All this drinking and smoking and womanising. He's not reliable any more."

"Shall we put him on your bed?"

"Put him on the floor near the window."

"I'm all right," I said.

"He's all right," Freville said, dropping me. "I'll get you a scotch, chum."

"Are you really all right, Mr Fenton?" the secretary asked me when he'd gone to the kitchen. Then she whispered urgently: "You've got to get away from him!"

It was the first time I had ever met her eyes. She really cared about me. She was about thirty, but never mind. From then on I felt there was a prisoner in the next cell and I only had to tap the wall. I don't remember her name.


This was the night we got the Rutland stone. I used to do anything rather than go home, sometimes. I met Diana again but I didn't know it was again. It's difficult to make this sound convincing. In fiction it's the kind of thing which would immediately be rejected as impossible. I've tried it, so I know. And two characters with the same name you mustn't use. My two children called Lang, for instance; or Diana the sculptress and Diana our Monster. You can always tell whether a story is true or not because in life you can know six people with the same name. And the same faces and the same minds.

The same with not recognising people, or roads. Unless it's just me. I met Edna at the firm's 1936 Christmas Party for instance. She smiled at me and immediately called me Horace. We went on from there. Friendly girls are not that frequent. Later in the night I was telling her about a girl I worked with on the coil-assembly line whose ears stank.

"That's me," she said.

That's how she knew my name, of course, and why she smiled at me. We worked together. She wasn't amazed or anything that I hadn't known. Edna was never amazed at

[61]

anything. We'd been working together for six months. I didn't even like her. Anyway, it was too late then, she was pregnant.

It gets you into trouble but also there's an advantage about this defect, if that's what it is: everything and everybody comes new to you.

"This wide-eyed-boy thing is your greatest asset," old Angie told me once. "You do it so well."

It is not an act.

Diana was one of my babbling club. When things got on top of me or I felt that I wasn't being treated as a writer, wasn't getting my share, there were about four people I could babble to over the glasses. There was old Angie at the library, Diana the Sculptress at the Palette Club in Soho, Cedric the editor of the Caxton Drake detective library and of course Albert the milk. There was an affinity, a sympathy, a tuned-in-ness, a mutual receptiveness; and in a life-time, four is not many.

We started off by babbling our whole life story and all our troubles but after that it was just a short babble, informing the status quo, bringing each other up-to-date. Each of the four suit a different mood and if they happen to meet oddly enough they don't like each other.

"What do you find to talk about with him?" they'd ask me.

Diana was at the Palette Club after a Norman Freville type day. At first I thought she wasn't there and I just drank. And then the life-class curtains opened and Diana came out and saw me. She screamed, is the closest I can get to what she does.

"Stay there, Horace! Don't go away! Don't start talking to anybody!"

And then what she did was go round and sit with five or six old men. She always did this. She had a kind of smudged beauty you get in old paintings. Classical features, long red hair, Baptist Chapel kind of robes about one hundred years out of date. I've seen her, I'm certain, in those coloured

[62]

bible-story illustrations. I don't know what she talked to these old men about but they seemed to expect it. She would talk quietly and earnestly, leaning to one ear or the other depending how they were deaf and with the blind ones she would rest a finger on them.

One of these old gentlemen, a well-known artist and just past the hundred mark, was being made the subject of a conducted tour while Diana was talking to him and she had to break it off and came back to me.

"He's in a mood," she said. And she said: "Now what about you? Did you get home all right?"

I thought she was talking about the last time we had babbled. She was talking about the Royal Film Première. I didn't know she was there so I went on talking.

"It must be seven months," she said. "No, nine months. Or more? You'd been offered a film. Has it come out yet?"

"Oh for God's sake don't talk about it. Did you see the summer?" To Diana I use this cryptic poetic chat.

"Petal we went to the Balearics. Did some heads. A rich American family. Caucasian primitives. You ought to go. Basil looks like a Greek god. He's marvellous."

You should start taking notes here. Basil was her brother. I gave her my last few summonses and the Spanish twist on the new picture and the big cheque I was waiting for from Freville.

"You shouldn't invest it with Albert," she said then.

I was shocked. The way you are when you're caught out in a lie or an exaggeration or another version of the truth. You're telling somebody something and you suddenly realise they've heard the same thing from somebody else.

"I didn't know you knew Albert?" I said.

"Well I didn't know *you* knew him until that night."

"What night?"

"The première," she said. Then she screamed again. "Oh Horace! You didn't know it was me!"

She had got it from my face which I now covered with my hand in my well-known way.

[63]

"I *thought* you were different," she said. "A different vocabulary. That's why I didn't say much. Not that I could move my face under all that make-up. I do forgive you, Horace. Even Basil didn't know me."

There was no coincidence here it was just the roads over again and the small diversion that suddenly connects; the bits of your life you didn't know were hidden by that row of poplars.

"So we both live in the same town?" I said.

"Well you know that!"

I didn't know that. All I knew about Diana were her work, her bills, her brother, her rock troubles. The two of them, brother and sister, besides carving their bread and butter in family portraits made Aztec gods and other strange enormous shapes whose ancestry, she said, was the genesis of the piece of rock from which it was formed.

Put simply, she said, you take a potato which reminds you of something and then work on it until the resemblance is stronger though not necessarily recognisable.

"We put in an extra shift for God," she told me.

I didn't know anything about her home town and she didn't know anything about mine; or my families and friends and relations and general geography. Diana was philosophy—old Angie was geography.

"What about the coffee-bar on Saturday mornings?" she said now.

This really hit me. In the High Street on a Saturday morning there were always these two kinky characters doing their shopping. From the back you would think they were two sisters, both with their hair down their backs, both in jeans, holding hands. From the front one was a man with a beard down to his chest. The girl I had tried to make passes at several times in the coffee-bar where they finished their shopping. It turned out that was Diana too and that was her brother Basil.

The simple answer is that when somebody is absolutely certain that you know everything then they don't bother to tell you. I had brought her into my own life without realising it. I had started off by making Albert a member of the Palette on the pretence that he was a theatrical agent (you had to be something in the arts) and he had got Diana in.

"You seconded my application-for-membership form," she told me now. I don't read forms. Albert was always engaged in personal exchange and mart as he fished for contacts and favours. Diana was curiously nervous now, almost frightened. "You're not fooling me, Horace?"

I told her that I wasn't. I reminded her about my weakness.

"I don't think it's that," she said, her eyes a bit too bright. She didn't explain it then.

Her mood had slipped. It wasn't the Palette Club babbling mood. It reminded me more of the time I had taken her back to Cedric's flat in Queensgate and tried to make her. If you talk to people a lot you can't make them, I'd found that out; but I tried anyway. The complicated idea was that we should go with Cedric to have some supper at the Air Terminal restaurant in Cromwell Road and then Cedric would slip me his key and make an excuse to join us later at his flat for drinks; that he would bring some friends in.

"But why!" he said to me in the lavatory. "Why don't you go for something normal? She's a bloody high priestess! I've met 'em boy, King's Road is full of 'em."

She had dropped some incense sticks out of her handbag in the restaurant. It wasn't just that. He had been listening to us talking.

"I've never seen you like this, Horace," he said.

He seemed really disappointed in me.

"Why don't we make love?" I asked Diana that night.

We were alone in Cedric's flat sitting on his bed drinking his beer and yet I had to wedge this suggestion into the conversation. She didn't hear it until about the third time.

"No, Horace," she said, simply. "If we did you would go away just the same and I couldn't bear that."

I tried one or two things but she was adamant.

[65]

"If we had a flesh relationship you'd have to stay with me for always," she said.

I persevered.

"Oh well, if you must," she said, just as simply and as if she'd tried to save me but had failed.

I couldn't do it. And when I had persisted for about ten minutes she got a fit of the giggles. I gave it up. When I came to think of it I couldn't imagine putting my hands on her breasts or her vagina; I mean you can't do that kind of thing when you're talking to somebody.

"Stop worrying, Horace," she said. "We possess each other without it."

It wasn't as much fun, that's all.

And now in the club after some more drinks and just as they were closing she said: "Do you know what I think, Horace? I think our relationship is strange and beautiful and outside our control."

There are some people who are always looking for somewhere to put the blame. I asked her why it was she had never asked me to drive her home if we lived in the same place.

"Neddy takes me," she said.

Neddy, about eighty, was standing inside the clubroom door holding her cloak. I didn't want her to go with him. It was the time of night when you look round desperately for what's left. Knowing her now in at least two other places our relationship had shifted a little. I thought I might even be able to do it.

"Let's drive to the coast?" I asked her.

More than anything, the fact that she knew Albert had killed some of my reverence. I was trying to remember if he'd put his hand on her the night of the première or spoken about her afterwards; if I'd heard anything about her in the High Street. If I could have destroyed her a little I reasoned I could do it.

"You really want to drive somewhere tonight, Horace?" she said.

Women, no matter how mystical, fated, strange and beautiful they may be, are always instant for the main chance. The rock was usually sent blind by railway and she paid by weight, mostly for the transport.

"If I could actually choose a piece while it was still in the ground, Horace!" It was like a long-frustrated would-be mother hearing about the first fertility pill.

"What would you do for me?" I asked her. This was more an old Angie question.

"Anything, Horace. Everything."

Funny how women start to feel safe once you've been impotent; start to take chances and get daring with you.

It was foggy. Not just local fog. There was a layer of dense ground fog one-hundred-and-sixty-five miles long that *I* could vouchsafe. We did a hundred miles up the wrong road and had to go across country. Even with a spot-light on the verge you get so that you think you are flying through cloud. You get isolated. Diana sang madrigals all the way in a piercing soprano voice.

A rather unpleasant thing happened at Loughborough on the A6. We were flagged by a woman who turned out to have a man with her. She was about forty and made up like a tart. He looked like a tramp.

"How far are you going?" I asked them.

"Not far," the woman said.

They got in the back seat and I started off through the fog again. Then gradually I began to feel the back of our seat vibrating. Diana noticed about the same time but pretended she hadn't. She wasn't singing with strangers in the car but she started a bright chat about Aztec religion.

"Who were the Aztecs, then?" I asked.

"They were an offshoot of the stone-boiling Indians who were the first inhabitants of the American continent."

They were having it off on my back seat. The fellow must have got one leg down on the floor with his foot under our seat giving him leverage and rhythm. I was hot, prickly with embarrassment. Albert has seen people do it but not me.

"Where did they come from then?" I asked.

"From Asia," Diana said, heartily, loudly, poor girl.

We were *moving*.

"Why call them stone-boiling Indians?" I asked, avidly.

"Because. . . ."

She stopped talking; we both stopped talking while they had their climax. It was not deference so much as paralytic horror.

"They used to heat their water by dropping red-hot stones in," Diana said tiredly.

"Just here, mate," the fellow said.

I stopped and I heard the chink of money and muttered thanks. The fellow got out and went into a thatched cottage fifty yards past the road that turns off the A6 (signpost Borrowash) just outside Derby. And I wish I could give his bloody name. The woman we dropped at some prostitute's broadway in Derby itself.

"Ta love," she said.

We had overshot our road by miles. You don't have to go to Derby to get to Rutland. We took the road to Billsdon, Uppingham, Dullington and Stamford. Neither of us mentioned what had happened.

You may think rock is rock. It isn't.

"Thart bit thar's no use," the old man said.

Picture the ancient standing on a miniature Grand Canyon with the red sun rising through the last of the fog behind him. It is a low shot from where Diana and I are standing and he looks like a bit of old grey rock himself.

"What's the matter with it?" I said.

"It's had the elements at it," he said.

"Elements?" I said.

"Ar—the wind the rain the sun and the air," he said.

I must have looked stupid but life is so complicated that when you are faced with the elements you don't know them. I picked up another piece.

"Not that piece!" Diana cried.

"That bit has lost its nature," the old man explained.

It gave me the shivers. Lost its nature? There was something diabolical about it. I thought of the germ of life, the gene itself, losing its own root and feeding instead on its environment, devouring what nurtured it, becoming a great steaming thing. Lost its nature?

"This piece," Diana said, breathlessly.

She was choosing the rocks as an artist chooses his colours; except that she was choosing shapes at well; she saw in these rocks as she pulled the earth from around them the beginnings of shapes which ended in her mind. I strolled away and left them to it. It was not my world. Diana, the old man and the rocks seemed to have an implicit understanding.

We slept in the car for a couple of hours and then she sang madrigals again all the way south. Diana's happiness was centred not in me but in the three hundredweight of half-created monsters crouching behind us.


As so often before, what started with a fight for my rights, a little rebellion against being unloved, finished with a long waste of time and petrol and money. From this came the guilt and with it the certainty of waiting disaster. Now I waited for it like a bill. Muckiest of all was my self-hate at letting some tart copulate where my children would be sitting soon.

I never felt like this when I'd been with old Angie. She was wholesome, somehow. I felt that I had done something clean and healthy. She used to hold my hand afterwards as if she was grateful; as if to let me know that she was still there and everything was all right. Of course it wasn't new any more. It didn't stop the world.

I got back to Tres's house at mid-day, an unshaven wreck with a yellow tongue and slimy teeth and yesterday's shirt. Tres was in the hall, just writing me a note before leaving. She had on her ridiculous straw hat with the saw-edge of grey hair under it; a heavy blue-serge coat which Albert's mother had given her and the defiant red-and-white cowgirl neckerchief to remind her that she had once been a writer. She gave me an "ugh!" look.

"The oldest Dorian Gray in the business," she said. "You look as though you've been drugging schoolgirls all night and interfering with them."

"What's happened in the meantime?" I said.

"Edna's father's died," she said.

She was on her way to get a train down there. Albert's mother was coming in to see to the children and the cats.

"I'll go," I said.

"Well I should think so!"

I was so tired. I borrowed a pound she'd got from the Post Office for the children's allowance and drove round to Albert's caravan to tell Mrs Harris not to come.

"Can you come in a minute, Horace?" Mrs Harris said.

She was a slim, dainty, north-country woman of about fifty-five and she was a widow. She was blunt, worldly, kind-hearted and compassionate. It didn't help me. The more qualities she had the worse it was. I got a half-hour lecture about what I was doing to my families and to Albert and to myself.

"Are you a man or an irresponsible child, Horace?" she asked me. "There's going to be a terrible tragedy in your family if you don't do something about it now," she said. She wouldn't tell me what it was although she seemed to know.

The only thing I remember saying was that a writer had to live otherwise he couldn't write.

"I know," she said. "You're the same as Albert. You're like two peas in a pod. You should both have learnt a trade as soon as you left school."

Sitting in Hanger Lane for what seemed almost the rest of the morning I vowed to get the three thousand pounds on this picture and then do what I had often resolved to do. Take some old manor house in East Anglia and put both families into it. Form a self-supporting community. Get Tres writing again. Have a couple of pretty *au pair* girls to

[70]

look after me. I could never avoid that last thought. It was compulsive. It was like using a four-letter word after you'd said your prayers. It cancelled it all out. I couldn't change and I couldn't change anything. It was glandular.

The last set of lights changed. We were released like greyhounds across Ealing Common and down to Kew Bridge, racing each other desperately, viciously, for something out of sight.

All the children were there watching Edna who sat watching the blank television screen and her father dead.

"You don't have to marry her, Horace," he'd said to me in nineteen-thirty-six. "She'll never be more than twelve years old." We'd seen him about three times since.

"I'm sorry, Edna," I said.

It jerked her alive. She tried to run away out of the room as she used to do if any of the children hurt themselves. I caught her and held her. It took all my will-power. I hadn't been able to touch her for many years. If she gave me a penny or a plate I carefully took it by the opposite edge and she knew it. She would put things down so that I could pick them up. But I held her now and all the children came round and held us and the grandchildren held them. We stood in the middle of the room like a rugby scrum.

Sue came in and stared at us: "And may the best man win," she said, in a North-country accent.

Edna put her face up, relieved: "Silly bugger," she said.

The mourning was over.

# 7

# Barefoot Across the Grass

THE IMPORTANCE OF THE NEXT SUBSTANTIAL CHEQUE grew as it always grew; judgment summonses loomed ahead, mortgage foreclosure, committal warrant for rates, ponderous threatening movements from the tax office and the National Insurance office and across it all a snowstorm of small bills accruing to both households and the car.

"Could you put down exactly what your commitments are?" the bank manager asked me.

"No," I told him.

He sometimes used to get a very efficient mood. He was certain my affairs were not as complicated as I made them appear when I tried to explain them. Then he would browse some more over my account and fall silent. When a cheque came in of any size I wrote on average twenty cheques a day to God knows whom.

"Who are they? Who are these people! We can't even read the names! Are you sure you're not paying bills for the people who had the house before you did? It was always changing hands. . . ."

How can anybody's personal telephone bill be one hundred and twenty-five pounds? That's five pounds a week! Do you know how much my electricity bill is per quarter—fourteen pounds. That's with immersion heater, cooker, washing machine, refrigerator, television, radio, electric blanket—yours is eighty-five pounds! What else can you possibly have? What is a twenty-five pounds search fee? Lost letters? Oh, for your car. Can't they search for your car at their own expense? You carry these people! One hundred and forty pounds National Health stamp plus fifty pounds fine and then God knows how many doctors' bills, dentists, vets. You are paying both ways, Mr Fenton. Or not paying.

"That's what my other bank manager says."

"What's your overdraft with him now?"

"He's frozen it at three thousand."

"Is he content with that situation?"

"I don't know, I'm not."

"I should think not! Your combined overdrafts are costing you ten pounds a week in bank charges alone."

"I know they are."

"And you're not paying it."

"No, I know."

"How are you going to get out of it, Mr Fenton?"

"I shall sell the film rights of my new novel. That's what I did last year. That twelve thousand pounds cleared all my debts and I had fifty pounds over."

"But you haven't paid any tax on it. You must owe them thousands!"

"I don't think so. My expenses are around one hundred pounds a week. I kept a tally that one week while I had an accountant. A hundred pounds a week expenses."

"But you haven't got a hundred pounds a week!"

"However much of it I haven't got, that's the amount I'm getting into debt every week."

"Can you prove it? Have you got any receipts?"

"No."

He covered his face for a moment.

"I tell you what I want you to do, Mr Fenton, purely as a temporary measure," he said. "I want you to give the bank the equity on your house as an additional security."

"I don't think we've got one." I couldn't imagine us

[73]

having anything valuable that we hadn't already sold.

"It's the difference between what you owe the building society and what the market value of the house is today."

"I've got a second mortgage on that," I said.

He was silent again. Then he said: "I wish you wouldn't do things without telling me."

"I usually have to do them in a hurry. Raising money is like calling the fire brigade in my house."

He sat and laughed. This is a weakness if you're a bank manager. He asked me about the second mortgage and decided that bearing in mind the upward curve of property values there ought to be an equity available of about four hundred pounds. I signed a document which he happened to have ready.

"The house is in your name, I take it?"

"No. My wife's. It was her mother's."

He tore the document up without anger.

"Ask her to come in," he said.

This was not going to be easy. What little Tres had she liked to keep in her name.

"Do you feel all right in yourself?" he asked me before I left.

"Not bad."

"How's the rupture?"

"It's all right."

"When is the new book coming out?"

"Soon," I said. I hadn't finished it.

"Will it be another resounding success?"

"Oh yes."

"I was telling my wife," he said, relaxing thankfully as I had, now that the essentials were over, "Mr Fenton is like a gold miner who has spent the proceeds of a rich claim before he's actually struck gold at all." He laughed at this again and so did I. Then seeing me out, he said: "Take good care of yourself. With ten thousand pounds of debt round their neck other men have securities in bricks and mortar, factories, fields of corn, livestock, export contracts—all you've got is what's inside your head."

Albert was waiting outside with his milk float. Wherever he sees my car he waits by it. His milk deliveries had gone to hell since he started the Irish thing.

"The Countess wants to see you urgently," he said.

He was evasive about how he came to be speaking to her but I suspect he had tried tapping her for finance or checking up that Norman Freville was really working to get the picture off the ground.

"I think she wants to make you an offer," he said.

"What kind of offer?"

"I don't know. She was asking me questions about your crummy families. Are you attached to them and so on. I told her they were attached to you. You could do worse than marry her, Horace. Shack up with her, anyway."

"I thought you said she's a prostitute?"

"They get plenty of money."

"And instead of giving me three thousand pounds, Freville shoots me?"

"Get the money first," Albert explained. "Knock off the broad afterwards while he's busy on the picture. She might want to come in on our club. Make a nice hostess. She knows the business after all."

"Did you ask her?"

"Not yet. I thought it better to wait and see what she's offering you. I've got some change for the call."

"I'll do it from home."

"And let Tres get her number? Tell my Mum? We don't want the vigilantes at this stage."

Tres was always tearing strips off suspect callers or sending pithy brush-offs to correspondents whose letters she'd opened for me. I'd written to an elderly male novelist admiring his last book and he'd written back a grateful, refined letter, inviting me to have tea with him. Tres got hold of it

[75]

and wrote and told him to keep his dirty filthy paws off her husband and do his fornicating in his usual London cess-pits and not bring the foul stench of it into her house.

"I told *her!*" she said, long afterwards, when I came across his letter as I cleared out the empty house.

"If you can get there," Albert said, "she's going to be in after nine o'clock tonight."

I told him I wanted a bath and an early night.

"This is no time for standing still, Horace. I'm doing my part."

He was researching Mary the Irish barmaid every night.

"You have to get them used to it," he said, bravely.

I sensed that he was having trouble with her.


Casting was put back. As soon as something is put back you go to see your agent about other work. When I went into his office his telephone was ringing and nobody there. I picked it up; I'm compassionate about ringing telephones, I've been the other end too often.

The operator announced a call from Hollywood. She asked me if I was my agent and I said I was. What I meant was that it was his office and I expected he was in the lavatory and why hold up the call for another two hours.

"Martin?" a girl's frantic voice said. "You've got to help me! Thugs have just broken into my house and they're threatening me! They've got guns! They want twenty thousand dollars! That's more than I've got to come after deducting the house, car, chauffeur, all the things the studio laid on. Martin I didn't *need* all these things! If they don't take up the option after this picture I'll come back bank-rupt!" She broke off to scream for somebody to put the gun away then came back: "I've told them I'm ringing you to arrange payment for them! They've been here an hour while I waited for this call. What am I going to do, Martin? They'll kill me!"

"Could you repeat that," I said. "He's just come in."

[76]

My agent took the telephone and listened for an equivalent time. As he listened he was pruning his finger nails. This meant taking the receiver away from his ear. In casual aside he said to me:

"How goes the script?"

I couldn't talk about it. At last he said:

"All right, darling, don't worry. Have you rung Sam? He *must* be there—it's three o'clock in the morning there. Did you give your name? Ah, I see. Have you got a through line to his place? Well I can tell you you have. Just turn that little black handle at the side and then let me speak to him —okay?"

There was a short delay and then he said:

"Sam? Hello, boy—Martin from London. Did I? I'm sorry. We forget the time. How's the picture going? Good. Good. Good. Is she? That's good. Ah, pity. Well if you take her up get her nose operated on for the next picture and do something about those ears! I agree. A very good voice— yes, and her laugh. I wouldn't touch that. Yes. Yes. Oh, and Sam—call the boys off. She's in to me for a thousand pounds —you've just about zeroed her now already. Okay? Thanks. No, don't put me back. 'Bye."

This agent was in, perhaps, Grosvenor Place. Everybody is waiting to slap a writ on you. To make your agent, as with others, you have to combine two or three old agents, preferably dead ones (I have outlived five). A number of my agents died and one went blind.

"Cheer up," I said, "it's not the end of the day, it's only lighting-up time."

I used to think you had to be clever to be a writer but you don't. You have to be clever to be a phoney.

"He wants me to do another picture," I told him. I was talking about Freville's threat.

"You're very lucky," my agent said. "Snap it up. I'm surprised that he's asked you. He's been complaining for a long time about your time-keeping."

It is easy and not very original to be disparaging about

agents but I would like to put in a word in their favour. They are out of touch yes—after five years my agent used to bungle my name, particularly after the arrival of Charles Fenton with his football story—but the writing and show-business world is not a bad world to be out of touch with. An agent has to present a respectable, sober, establishment front to all parties and particularly to solicitors; he may be selling a drug-ridden homosexual homicidal incestuous freak, but he must do it in terms of legal integrity and dinner at the Dorchester.

The fixed smile an agent wears is the smile the man in the snake-pit has to turn to his audience.

"What about television?" I asked him.

"Would it be good for your name?" he said. "You haven't lived down those boys' adventure stories yet."

He had the mistaken idea that the Caxton Drake library was juvenile.


I went down to Fleet Street and looked up Cedric in his little tin office. It dismayed me to find now that the Caxton Drake library had folded they had put him to work on a Hereward the Wake comic. It was like finding a noble animal in captivity. He was a big, heavy, intellectual man with serious politico-social interests which hadn't seemed to come to anything yet. He had put up once as a parliamentary candidate; his rival had got almost one hundred per cent of the votes. Cedric had been stoned. His top lip had been cut by a brick and he had grown a heavy old-fashioned moustache to hide it. It had affected his speech slightly and he had a tooth which he had to keep pushing back.

"Well Horace!" he said. "This *is* nice."

He hadn't always thought so. He used to love my writing and buy it but it got him into trouble. I used to plot my Caxton Drake stories so that I could chop out the detective afterwards and publish them in hard covers and sell film rights. Caxton Drake enthusiasts sometimes couldn't find him at all he was so incidental. I cut down the readership by fifty per cent and shifted the age group. Cedric also got the political bit between his teeth and other writers followed with sex and religion. On some of the last issues they were still advertising "Be A Ventriloquist" kits on *Sons of War and Peace*.

He offered me the Hereward the Wake comic strip at a pound a page which I turned down.

"I don't know why you don't cannibalise more of your old Drakes," he said. "That's what I'm doing. There're paperbacks starting every week and they're crying for good meaty stuff. I've sold two of mine to the Sex And Religion series. I'll introduce you to the editor. He's a fruit but he'll buy anything you stick under his nose when he's tight. Why don't you do it, Horace? Three hundred pounds each plus a royalty if and when."

"It wouldn't be good for my name, now," I told him.

He took a white towel and a scrap of soap out of his drawer and went to wash his hands. He did this hand-washing all through the day; it was more a comment than a necessity.

Later across the road in the Cogers we had some Guinness and a little babble.

"Look at me," he said. "I've got a new suit. You could have a new suit, Horace. You think too much about your bloody name since you switched to hard-covers. Your place in literature. I'll tell you something, Horace, and old Tres will bear me out—your best writing is in those Caxton Drakes. Yes, you've got a nice line in literary crap now but how many readers? How much money? With Caxton Drake you had a hundred thousand readers clamouring for you—especially after *Innocence in Peril*. The writing you did for Drake was stylish and subtle. You know why? Because you made it up. You didn't go around with your little note-book mind f—— verity-reporting all your f—— pals. The Alcock picture was Drake writing, Horace, and the rubbish you do now—oh yes, the critics like it and

[79]

everybody says how clever—is shit. It makes me sick, Horace. You're really such a good writer." He pushed his tooth up. "There was poetry in those Drakes."

"Now how about you, Cedric?" I said.

"I'm sick," Cedric said, "of Fleet Street. I'd like to freelance like you Horace. Run barefoot across the grass."

"I should think very carefully about it first," I told him.

He grinned at me. Whenever I said anything that sounded sensible or like something somebody else would say, my friends knew I was drunk. He punched me.

"Give me a breakdown, you literary bastard!"

But I'd got a date, I'd just decided.


"I'm a prostitute."

"I don't believe you," I lied.

She was sitting at the opposite end of the bath tickling my genitals with her toes. Even in this she was graceful, ladylike, feminine, aristocratic. There was nothing bold or brazen about it for this, as she knew perhaps better than I, would have offended me. On a cork-topped stool next to the bath was an expensive, gold-leaf decorated volume of French poetry. She had been reading from it, while I washed her, a poem about a courtesan at the court of Louis the Fourteenth. Her remark about being a prostitute was a claim more than a confession; a moment of reflected glory.

"It's more tasteful and more moral than having a string of rich marriages and a life cluttered up with trophies and scalps and fatherless children."

"What was so urgent?" I asked her.

Nothing we had done since I got to her flat had seemed remotely urgent; pleasant, but not urgent.

"Those lovely peasant feet," she said.

She moved her breast against one of my feet and traced her finger up and down the roadways of my veins.

[80]

"And yet you don't appear to be a proletariat writer. You have too much humour."

"On my mother's side," I told her, "we come from a French Countess and her gardener."

"And your father's?"

"Policemen, tanners and builders."

"It's a nice, unlikely mixture. No writers?"

"No published writers that I know about. My grandfather was a lay preacher. I was named after Spurgeon, the baptist preacher. We used to shoot airgun pellets at his portrait. My mother collected Patience Strong poems which she stuck all over the walls."

I have an urgent need sometimes to tell people about myself.

She thought about this while she ran in some more hot water. "I'm thinking of adopting you," she said then, "that's why I'm asking you all these questions."

At one end of this magnificent bath was an expanse of pink marble which was covered in the most beautiful bottles and jars of cosmetics and various hygienic-looking things that you see in hospitals.

"How would you like to come to Italy with me?"

"I couldn't. I haven't got time."

I hadn't got time to go to prison, I hadn't got time to be ill, or die.

"To Rome," she said, stroking me again.

"I couldn't possibly. I'd love to but I couldn't."

"I run two flats in Rome." She said "run" in a casual but businesslike manner like Albert talking about companies. "Then I have a permanent chalet on the coast about three-quarters of an hour from Rome. The trees grow right down to the beach. Is that a rupture?"

I laughed. "Don't do that!" Old Angie used to do that.

"Of course I would settle all your bills."

"That would take ten thousand pounds," I was now able to tell her.

This is really why I had come to see her, I told myself.

I hoped that her urgent news might have something to do with money; people get to know that the only urgent thing in a writer's life is money. Even drunk I wouldn't have had the courage but for Albert telling me that Freville had gone to Ireland to see a girl shooting on location who he thought might make a Pilar.

"Ten thousand?" she said. "I'm glad. You seemed to me the sort of chap who was worrying about the odd thirty bob."

"It's largely made up of odd thirty bobs," I said.

"Do you like this?" she asked.

"Yes."

She smiled at me. "You're so relaxed already and only the second time. Promise me you won't ever get blasé, Horace, or I shall lose interest in you. I'd like to plough something back into literature and the arts. That's what *she* did." She indicated the book without stopping what she was doing. "It's a justification, I suppose."

"Plenty of writers and artists about," I said.

"I want you," she said, distinctly.

"I've got two families."

"You are not involved with them. You can't be or you wouldn't have two. You love them and you will care for them but you are not involved with them."

"I don't know."

"I'm telling you, Horace."

It's true she seemed to know quite a lot about me.

"Your only true allegiance is to your talent," she said.

Horace Spurgeon Fenton, writer, artist and year-book, I thought.

She said: "You have the arrogance which comes from that. Whatever their sufferings—be it wife, mistress, child, girl-friend, brother or whatever—you feel that they are privileged to be a part of your life because it gives them, in return for this pure accident, a place in English letters. Forever."

"Yes—no!" I said. Nobody could be as conceited as

[82]

that. It didn't sound conceited the way she said it. It sounded very nice.

"Do you know about the mess of Balzac's life?"

"Yes."

"Dickens' harsh wife and little shop girl?"

"Yes."

"Maupassant?"

"Yes."

"Why?"

"What?"

"Why?"

"I happen to have read them."

"You happen to have read about all the great writers who you deeply believe had the same kind of life that you have, the same kind of sufferings, the same kind of bitchy women and dependent oafs."

"No!"

"Yes! And Fitzgerald? Do you know about him?"

"Yes."

"*What Makes Sammy Run?*"

"Yes—Schulberg."

"*The Last Tycoon?*"

I admitted it.

"*The Whiteoaks Saga?*"

"Good God no!"

"Cronin?"

"Certainly not!"

"Amis?"

"No."

She was laughing. "Come to Rome."

"I couldn't."

"Come and write your books. That's all you want to do. To write them you would sacrifice everybody—admit it."

"I don't know."

"Every book is a monument erected to yourself."

There was a kind of phallic relevance about this and

what she was doing. "You wait to see which one will stand. Who burns doesn't matter a damn."

We made love under water and then she dried me.

"You can make them an allowance, fly to see them whenever you like. They'll be happy, provided for and clear of debt."

"I couldn't do it, Jane."

"There's another summer waiting for us out there," she said.

She knew that I had just lost one.


I ran out of petrol seven miles from home at half-past two in the morning. I don't know about leaving them for good I could never stay away from them all night if I was within striking distance. I'd get up and get dressed and get out no matter who it was. I liked to be sure everybody was all right at home, I liked to be at Tres's when she fed the cats and got the children off to school; or next to that at Edna's to cheer them off to work.

I walked the last two miles carrying my shoes. There was a petrol station open not far from the car but I hadn't enough money for even one gallon. And my lovely peasant feet have lovely peasant corns. I cut them every few days with a razor blade.

There was a strange man asleep on the settee when I went in—that would be about four o'clock. I had a job waking him up; I think I'm too diffident.

"Mr Fenton?" he said when he was sitting up.

A homely middle-aged chap with an old-fashioned detached collar which he'd undone. He got up and shook hands. "I'm Mr Simpson. I came to collect the car again. I was at the other place last week and the week before that here. Did your wives tell you? I seem to keep missing you. I cut the lawn for your missus tonight and then got stuck in front of the television and then I thought I might as well wait for you. Could I have the keys?"

I told him the car was in London.

"Oh dear," he said.

I used to lie to keep my car.

"I had a crash," I said. "It won't be any use to you."

"You couldn't let me have eighty-five pounds, could you?" he asked. He knew I couldn't. "Twenty?"

I offered him a post-dated cheque. I issued so many post-dated cheques that I could pay a thousand pounds in on a Monday and it would be gone by Friday without my spending a penny.

"They're wise to that one," he said. "You'd better just let me have the location of the car and then it's up to them."

I can invent ten thousand words a week but never a false address. I gave him Cedric's address.

"Is that your guitar upstairs?" he asked. "I've been having a bit of a browse round."

I told him it was.

"Could you give us a tune?"

I took him up to my room and played one of my blues on the Epiphone.

"Do I know it?" he asked.

I told him I only played my own stuff.

"What about that painting? Your missus says you did it."

I agreed.

"So if you want a tune you make it up," he said, "and if you want a painting for the wall you paint it?"

"That's right."

He absorbed this and then laughed. "You're a character, you are, Mr Fenton. Pity you didn't make your own bloody car, eh?"

I saw him out. He had parked his car in the garage. As I came in I remembered that my asthma inhaler was in my car seven miles away. It was my habit to keep it in the cubby hole so that I was never caught without it either end. I got asthma immediately. Badly. I woke up Tres and told her. She got up and telephoned the police station; she would never get taxi drivers out of bed. Not that I could

[85]

have afforded it then. Tres got something on and came with me to the hospital in the police car. Lewis was left to make coffee for us.

Sandra was on night duty. Pretty and sexy but hard as nails. She took me into a cubicle and left Tres sitting in the outpatients. A young yob-type doctor came and gave me one of the new aerosol inhalers and then left me to it. Sandra had a horrifying line in small talk about operations, deaths, diseases, accidents. Somewhere near somebody was calling out occasionally.

"That old cow keeps on and on," the Sister said.

This is total recall. She went on chatting about a barbecue she had been to and all the doctors who wanted to make her and the jealous rages she had ignited since coming there. My chest was easing off but I kept using the aerosol, not knowing yet it was the wrong one. That it was attempted murder.

"So anyway this kid was brought in and Ted wouldn't come near her because he was still wild with me about Saturday night so I cut open her chest and massaged her heart and she recovered—Ted was livid! He doesn't like you. Did you hear him? 'Funny he always gets asthma when you're on,' he said. Well he found out about that weekend at Brighton—it was you, wasn't it?"

I love this "it was you wasn't it" thing from people who live such full lives they can't remember who they've lived them with.

It was me as it happens.

It was the most awful weekend I've ever spent; blood, wombs, guts, eyes, brains, human offal for two whole days and nights.

I tried to write it into a story called *Dirty Weekend* for the Caxton Drake series but hadn't the stomach for it.

She raped me on the Friday night as soon as we got there. She'd got hold of some purple hearts and tried to get me to take some which I wouldn't. God knows what they did to her. There was a time during the night when I thought

[86]

she was killing me. She did it about five different ways non-stop almost and just as though I wasn't there except as part of a device which she needed. I lay flat on my back with my arms spread out, not taking part, while she flounced up and down first on her stomach and then actually sitting on me with her back towards me and holding the bottom bedrail as if in a rowing machine.

Every now and then she stopped to apply a kind of artificial respiration—she had all these tricks for keeping the condition right. I was frightened, to be honest. For a time I was afraid she would have a heart attack but soon that I would. I'm sure that's how I got the rupture. It's only at times like that I remember I'm not forty any more.

"I shouldn't stay long," she told me now, "Ted's got a filthy temper."

This was when I realised that he had given me the wrong aerosol. My heart was pumping so much that everywhere I touched the bed, my buttocks, my arms, my feet, I could feel a sledge-hammer going. I tried to sit up and almost passed out.

"Get my wife." I said.

"She's not allowed in here," she said.

I wanted to call for help. It took me half an hour to persuade her to give me some aspirin to try to counteract the drug. What the doctor had given me was the inhalant designed for real asthma, bronchial asthma, the kind they recognise. And being an aerosol instead of my far less concentrated hand spray I had taken ten times too much.

"You wouldn't have had any claim on them," Tres told me afterwards.

She meant if I'd died. She was so right. I could just imagine the sex-pot sister bragging about it as another conquest. "Do you know what Ted's done now?" The screams had stopped by the time I left.

"I don't know why they always have to peg out when I'm on duty!" Sandra grumbled.

And yet these are the very people who can say: "Good morning, lovely now!" fluently.

Tres frightened me on the way home. The police car never waited for us; it was only about a half-mile distance.

"Freville telephoned," she said.

"He's in Ireland!"

"Don't shout at me," she said. "He wants as much as you've done of the script and everything to do with it. Any old writing, I suppose he means."

"What's happened, then?"

"I don't think anything's happened. I don't expect it ever will."

Norman Freville and his gun had been about a two minute car ride from the Countess's flat. He was probably with her now. I guessed she'd tell him I'd been there, too; she was the type.

"That means London again tomorrow."

She didn't answer.

"Have you got enough for me to get a can of petrol and take a bus out to the car in the morning?" I asked her.

"If I had," Tres said, "I'd buy Fiona a pair of plimsolls and let the poor little devil go to school."

I felt like a failure.

Albert's milk float rattled past the end of our road and I held back to avoid him.

I'd never actually done this before, but I hitch-hiked to London the next day. I got a lift in a Co-op lorry to Hatfield, passing my abandoned car on the side of the road; then a Shredded Wheat lorry stopped for me and took me as far as Hendon Central. I had just enough cash for a tube train down to Marble Arch. I was carrying a pile of script. (One day I'll get a briefcase.)

Freville's flat was untidy in the way that a fight makes

it untidy. Furniture had been overturned and replaced in the wrong places. The secretary had gone home. Norman Freville lay on his scarlet couch calling me to come in when I was already in. There was an excitement about him.

"Fix yourself a drink, chum." This was excitement.

"Thanks."

"How's the script?"

"Marvellous." You have to be definite, or they'll say when they've ripped it to pieces, "Even you weren't too satisfied with it."

"I'm going to get an independent deal on it after all," he said. Everything in this line was between the lines.

I sat down with a neat scotch.

"I don't have to be dictated to any more," he said.

I had the feeling you get when you go into a cinema as they're playing *God Save the Queen*.

"What happened?"

"Better still," he said, "from your point of view especially, it doesn't have to be set in Spain."

There was a short pause while I considered this.

"I always thought that ruined it," he said, after some artistic contemplation. "You thought that too, didn't you?"

"It didn't improve it."

"You're absolutely right, chum," he said.

He was doing it again. Getting me on his side before I knew what side he was on.

"Luckily," he said, "I've got my own end money. We can pick and choose who we make it with."

There was the first "we". Any ghastly blunder and he would associate me with it as if it gave it some authority.

"This is really the way I wanted it, Horry old boy," he said, getting back to that pre-deal intimacy. "I haven't been truly happy since I flew to Hollywood."

"What's happened?" I said again.

There was a broken glass under the radiogram.

"Those bastards . . ." He mentioned the big American company which was not Paramount who were backing the

[89]

Hollywood star's salary in return for U.S. and overseas distribution and something that always sounds like "Passe Partout". "Do you know what they wanted?"

I didn't know. I only knew the film had fallen through.

"They wanted script approval!" he said.

Script approval! Everybody in the business has script approval, who cares who else has it? The actors have it, the extras have it, the camera-lighting man has it, the production secretary who puts in her own dialogue and the continuity girl who pulls a face at something and the man on the sound boom who shouts: "I've got a better line there!" I have re-written dialogue on location that has been contributed by a nearby ice-cream man. "That's a good line, Horace—did you hear that? Horace! Horace, get this down before we forget it—thank you, sir!"

"Script approval?" I said.

"Did you ever hear anything like it? For their measly hundred thousand pounds!"

"Shouldn't we accept?"

"For God's sake! They'd pull the balls out of it! Castrate it! Have you seen an American Housewive's League of Purity and Virginal Behaviour and no cock before forty?"

"What?"

"They censor shit out of it. Even the horse would need trousers never mind your dialogue—No! We'll preserve our artistic integrity. We'll get another star—for less money. We shall make this picture our way, old chap."

He had come back from Spain and America and was English independent again.

"Solly can go to hell," he said.

"What did he say?"

It was Solly's Company that had paid for the story and script so far, plus the Spanish expenses and whatever other things were involved.

"He swore at me," Freville said. "I hit him."

Agents, as I say, need to be apart from all this.

I said: "I won't get the first half of the split payment for final script, then?"

Norman Freville closed his eyes and crossed his hands on his stomach as he lay on the scarlet couch.

"I have withdrawn the subject," he said.

There was a hint of power and achievement in it.

# 8

# Lewis

THE PUPIL WROTE TO HIS TUTOR on the large blue oblong
sheet of correspondence-school reply paper.

*Dear Mr Fenton,*

*Thank you for your criticism of the last little effort.
I quite see what you mean.*

*I hope you find the enclosed more to your taste. I
should tell you that it was originally published in*
Onward, *our Parish Magazine, and got a special mention by the Vicar in a sermon delivered in front of the
Bishop of Bath and Wells. I realise that this does not
put it in the professional class but I hope you think
after reading it, "My goodness, he will be, by and by!!!"
Any how, see what you think.*

*You will be interested to know that I read out the
best pieces of your remarks about the novel I started
during the war while looking after "Sammy" (the horrible barrage balloon you may remember). They all
thought it was jolly good too. I mean the Literary
Society of which it is my honour to be honorary Secretary (unpaid!!!) this year. If I manage to get the
report of the meeting accepted by John O'London's
I will send you the cutting which I actually worded
myself. I wish you would let me mention your name
though I quite realise it is not the done thing.*

*As you say, my metior seems to be in the third person
story where I don't have to put so many "I's". I really
lost myself in the one to hand and parts of it made me
actually cry myself when I read it. I expect you know
what I mean. . . . It is funny how the characters seem
to take hold of your plot (one's plot, rather) and gallop
away with it so that you don't even know yourself what
is coming next. This type of style is more likely to give
you the famous O'Henry twist ending. (In my humble
opinion.)*

*But enough about the author as a person though I
do realise that this is what one has to get on to the
paper. I would be very much obliged if you would give
me one of your special criticisms of the accompanying
morsel. Would it fit the* Evening News *do you think
(it is 1,263 words) or is it too controversial?*

*I look forward as always to your reply and getting on
with the next lesson (rhythm and atmosphere).*

*Yours truly,*

*(Richard Oswald Thompson)*

*P.S. Willie ("Happiest Daze of His Life" you remem-
ber) saw one of your pictures at the local flea-pit.
He says it is really excellent stuff.*

*P.P.S. Will you be back for good now? They keep put-
ting me onto another tutor (W. Briggs) who does
not really understand what I am getting at.*

To this pupil and half a dozen like him I replied at
waffling length and with wet sincerity encouraging them
to abandon their wage-slave occupations and run barefoot
across the grass. I got two pounds for each lesson.

Tutoring for a writing school, writing copy and visuals
for an advertising agency (DON'T JUST STAND THERE—the
call for blood donors), reading and synopsising books for
film companies, taking the odd porno-editing job (an
orgasm every four pages, Gladys, or you're out) working as

[93]

a part-time P.R.O. for a Do-It-Yourself firm (how to turn soap powder cylinders into a gay maypole for your Christmas decorations) and fiction reading for magazines. These were the dry-season jobs of a writer's life.

When a film had fallen through at the most profitable option stage leaving me stuck for thousands and unable to face the banks or tell the manager that the golden prospects of next Tuesday had suddenly vanished then I had to pick up small, day-by-day Friday-by-Friday money fast. I went around to old chums I had been snubbing during the good days and knocked on the doors, pulling my forelock.

"You're joking you must be!" the woman secretary of the correspondence school said.

"That girl was heading for trouble," I said. "If it hadn't been me it would've been somebody else."

It was always a terrible hazard. Some girls will do anything to break into print. Falsify their ages, dress like adults, tell you their parents know they're spending the weekend in London. The whole thing was a tissue of lies and it put me the closest I've ever got to the Sunday papers.

"You know she nearly died?" the woman secretary said.

Cedric had found somebody he swore was reliable but you can't trust anybody. Fortunately it put him in it almost as deeply as I was. He kept it out of the courts by getting one of her short stories published in one of his firm's girls' magazines. I had practically to re-write it in one four-hour session in his office while he kept the girl's father drinking over at the Cogers.

"And do you think this is good for your name?" my agent had recently quibbled. He was holding a copy of the strip comic which, of all those on the market, his son had to read. It had my fifth Hereward the Wake story in it.

"By Horace Spurgeon Fenton!" my agent said.

It wasn't that bad. I had done the fall of Ely when Hereward the Wake knocked William the Conqueror's men into the marshes and watched them drown in mud, only finally to suffer dreadful defeat after Eric the Traitor had shown the barons the secret paths across the swamps. I did the Zulu war and The Ghost Squadron and then was back to my pupils.

"Back to your dirty little pen club?" Tres asked me, fairly pleasantly, when she found me working at the pupils' courses.

She had been in on the whole thing through opening every item of correspondence that came into the house. She had seen the first mild queries about syntax from D. H. Bognor Regis burgeon into the later desperate priority telegrams: *"Please send hundred pounds immediately love Dorothy."*

I was in the middle of my lesson to Richard Oswald Thompson when the bailiff brought a young girl in and introduced her as his wife. He was a retired policeman of about sixty and you'd have thought the Quickly was about as much as he could manage.

"It was through you we met," he confessed. "Maureen was reading one of your books in the County Court office—that's where she worked—and I saw her crying over it. 'I know that chap,' I said, 'He's one of my regulars.'"

The girl said: "I kept on at Bert to bring me round to see you."

"'Next time I've got a summons,' I said," the bailiff said.

"What kind of summons?" I asked him. It was the first I'd heard about another summons.

"I hope you don't mind," the girl said. "It must be terrible to keep getting interruptions."

I told her how to write a novel, got them some tea, accepted the judgment summons and the two-and-ninepence for my fare to court.

"Don't let it slip, Horace," the bailiff warned me, "or you'll go inside."

I watched her adjusting her skirt on the back of the Quickly and I heard the bailiff say:

"What did I tell you? That's the way to live, Maureen."
The judgment summons was for the eighteenth.


Albert came in about midnight when I was cooking Chitterlings to myself and whistling to Jimmy Dorsey clarinet solo from Red Nichols Five Pennies *Back Beat*. It's a ritual you can only master if you like chitterlings. Albert recoiled in horror, holding his nose. You got used to his exaggerated reactions.

He had news, he claimed, which was both good and bad.

"Mary's got her three sisters to come in," he said. "I'll put up their fare and buy them some clothes."

He showed me photographs while I ate. That seemed good. Then he told me that the vicarage had gone. That was bad.

"That's good really," he said. "I'm negotiating for The Grange. It's bigger and more isolated. There won't be any trouble with the neighbours about music and so on. I was thinking of having one of the new electric organs put in."

He asked me if I'd heard anything from Freville and I hadn't. I didn't expect to.

"Columbia will jump at it," Norman Freville had said when I left him for the last time.

Producers' offices are crammed with subjects that people were going to jump at. They lie there awaiting the Resurrection or Pay-TV, whichever comes first.

"I still think it will go," Albert said, "and I tell you why. The Countess has got twenty thousand pounds end-money of Norman's to keep it away from the tax people. When you've got that you're halfway home."

I was thoughtful enough not to ask him how he knew. Whether he had been trying to get himself adopted.

"She keeps it in a leopard-skin travelling case at the bottom of her wardrobe," he said.

He didn't go in for crime but sometimes I got the feeling that he was hoping I'd encourage him to.

"She's always out," he said.

I never dare pick it up, especially when we were down to chitterlings.

"If she invested a quarter of that," he said, "she'd have it back and with a profit by the time he needs it. The trouble is he keeps popping in!"

He brooded for a little while on something unpleasant that had probably happened.

"I don't like Freville," he concluded.

I liked him. You get the person in one line or one gesture, sometimes. The rest is you.

Edna had said: "I like the smell of earth."

Solly Corby had said: "I'm really a composer, you know, Horace."

A tycoon producer who thought I had a Scott Fitzgerald complex used to keep shifting around to keep the sun in his own eyes while we were talking.

And Norman Freville had put a hand on my shoulder one day when I was talking about the Monster: "It's a vale of tears, Horace," he said.


Tres had one of her recurring nightmares when I was washing up. I went up and broke it for her. As I came out of her room my son Lewis came from his, pyjamas twisted, his watchman's eyes instant for trouble.

"Is everything all right?" he said.

I told him it was.

"What's the time?"

"Three o'clock."

"Phew," he said. Then he said, gratefully: "I didn't know you were in, dad."

I gave him a hug. I couldn't talk to him. No money makes me more sentimental than anything else. I wondered how he handled things when I wasn't there.

"Go to bed when I go to bed," he used to mutter when we were trying to get him off to sleep as an infant. "Go to sleep when I go to sleep. Wake up when I wake up. See me in the morning."

I turned the tape to some Blue Four jazz. It always gave my sadness a setting. They were putting a straw hat on their troubles too and watching people dance to them.

# 9

# Fiona

Fiona broke the drought.

Instead of going to school the next morning she telephoned Arturo Conti's home though I didn't know this
until afterwards. I don't know who the hell else she telephoned now I come to think of it. She drifted into my room
about eleven and said she'd been sent home sick.

"You'd better go to bed," I told her.

"Yes," she said.

She started browsing through my tea-chest full of manuscripts, film scripts, stories, rejects, tear-sheets, loose
papers.

"You don't want to read that stuff," I told her.

"What are you doing?" she asked.

She hadn't made any really friendly overtures to me
since I let her and the class down by getting to the première
too late to shake the queen's hand. It wasn't the queen,
anyway; it was a poor relation.

I told her I was sitting there rehearsing how I could
con a few pounds from the bank manager.

"Why don't you sell some of your old stories?" she asked.

"It takes time."

"Why don't you cannibalise your Caxton Drakes?" she
said.

They got all this sort of chat from just being around. I
told her how long it would take to do and how long it would

take to find a publisher and then wait for payment. It would be like sending the key man in the bucket chain for the fire brigade.

"Haven't you got a good comedy would turn into a first class movie?" she said, unconsciously using Italian though I didn't then appreciate it. She left out Arturo's four-letter adjective, that was all.

"Plenty," I said.

"Not plenty," she said, "one. Name one."

I couldn't name one. I've always had a haystack of comedies. Everything is a comedy. Everything is the same comedy. She was getting tetchy. Livid.

"So if I rang you up and I was a film producer and I asked you for a comedy you couldn't name one?"

It was true.

She said: "What about that one about that girl who keeps getting tied up on the rug?"

I couldn't remember.

She took a deep breath and said it because there was no alternative: "The Virgin Prostitute!"

I blushed.

"Vicky read it," Fiona said. "She told me about it."

You and who else? I thought. Vicky was a year younger than she was.

"Would that make a first class f—— movie?" she asked. "I mean movie?"

"Make a marvellous film. Not in this country though. Filth needs a delicate touch to make it witty."

"You don't write filth, dad," Fiona said. I thought it was a compliment until she added with the exasperation of much wasted browsing: "I don't think you *can*." I remember thinking she didn't seem very sick.

The telegram came an hour later—What am I talking about? There was no telegram. I am so slow with some things. Her mother came in and spent half-an-hour moaning about the money situation, showing me new letters. From The Central Register of Defaulters:

*Dear Sir,*

*We have been advised by the above that in spite of applications by them you have defaulted in payment of your account.*

*Therefore* TAKE NOTICE *that failure by you to make a payment* DIRECT *to this* CREDITOR *within the next* SEVEN DAYS *may result in your name being registered as a* DEFAULTER *both locally and nationally. This registration will stop you obtaining any further credit in future.*

Six or seven like that (solicitors invented SEVEN DAYS, not God) and one from Edna:

*Dear Horace,*

*That chaps trying to take the radiogram now.* PLEASE *do something quick. You cant stretch seven pounds too weeks if you know it or not. Lang (boy) is in bed with tonsalitus (well you spell it!) Lang (girl) coming dinner tomorrow. Christ knows what Im supposed to give them. Cant you do something quick? Did you see your old picture on television? Mr Fortin liked it he said. Fiona has got a bicycle Im told. Funny init? She gets things without hafting to go office scrubbing. Her, I mean.*

*Yours truly,*

*Edna.*

"For God's sake get her a second-hand bike the next bit of money you get," Tres said. "She can have half of those eggs Albert brought."

At this time I would take anything we could get on tick down to Edna and anything she could get on tick up to Tres, ploughing backwards and forwards like an efficiently-employed cargo boat. There were no unemployment benefits for the freelance, no sickness pay and there still isn't. National Assistance I wouldn't touch. I was brought up on National Assistance, on parcels of clothes from the NSPCC.

(I sold it to *Best of the Year's Short Stories*). It would be like going back.

"Fiona says there are some good corsets at the school jumble sale. Headmaster's wife's. She could get them for about two shillings."

"Well for God's sake surely we've got two shillings?"

"If you don't mind breast of mutton."

"I don't give a sod," I said.

"Do you have to swear?" she said.

I wanted to get rid of her. My mind was ticking around *The Virgin Prostitute*, which was the object of the whole mother-daughter operation this morning.

You have these good stories which don't quite go and they lie neglected forever while you starve. I had published it as a Caxton Drake but then I had extracted it as a short film treatment which I couldn't get anybody to appreciate. It was too original.

The basic idea was that there is so much perversion, deviation, kinkiness about these days that it results in a kind of innocence. That a girl (I called her Orchard) wishing to prostitute and make a lot of money could cash in on this; could use whips, leather trousers, rubber boots, get tied up and everything else without ever losing her virginity. A good high-comedy idea. But could anybody see it? Well Fiona could, obviously; she was only ten but she'd got good taste. Anyway, try to keep children separate from what makes them and keeps them and you're saving up trouble for them.

Tres had this corny B-picture trick of delivering a punch line (Oh, and by the way) as she got to the door.

"Oh and by the way," she said. "There was a telegram from that Italian producer."

This whole scene had been to soften me up so that I would accept anything he'd got to offer. She wouldn't normally come and beef about the status quo when I couldn't change it. And then calling Arturo an Italian producer as though she was vague about him; he was the one and only person in the film business she liked. The rest she couldn't stand. She was intolerant. There was no one line and one gesture stuff about Tres.

"He wants you to ring him," she said, and went quickly.

I jumped up and ran slap into the wall. Working first here and then there I didn't know where I was half the time. At night if it was dark and I woke up with asthma I nearly fell out of the window more than once. And in the street I'd stop at traffic lights when I was walking.

"Horace?" Arturo said. "How are you?"

"Fine," I said.

"You lying bastard," Arturo said.

It was good to hear him. I was clearing my throat for him already (he had a thick, wheezy voice).

"Have you got a comedy would make a first-class effing movie?" he asked me. "I want it today and the money's waiting."

"How much?"

"Two hundred for an option."

I told him I had got one but that Sherek had asked me to write it as a stage play. I had lunch with a big theatrical impresario one day and he had suggested I write a play. I knew I would never do it. I don't get the right idea. There's only one kind of stage play. Every play you see is about a medium-sized room with one wall missing.

"Two hundred in fivers and don't tell anybody," he said.

"You may not like it."

"I will like it," he said. "What is it?"

I gave him *The Virgin Prostitute* in brief with some of the best sub-plots. The romance angle was also original. Orchard had been told by a fortune teller not that she would marry a tall dark handsome man but that she would marry Harry Kemble.

"Who's Harry Kemble?" she says.

The fortune teller didn't know either. It was the start

[103]

of her search which ended on Dartmoor. She waited five years for him to come out of jail. Then she had to convince him and he wasn't superstitious—a lot of stuff like that. Caxton Drake himself only came into the original because Harry was supposed to have his share of a two-million pound robbery stashed away. In fact what had happened was that he let people believe this in order to cash in on the corruption of the world and get himself re-established but the first bed scene with Orchard trying to convince him about horoscopes the camera pans away to the usual passion thing of waves breaking on rocks with the difference that out of the sea comes Harry's old oppo looking like Robinson Crusoe, a fish in one hand and a razor in the other, and we discover that he is marooned with the money on a desert island. This was as good as I could make it on the telephone, putting threepence in every three minutes. There was a good payoff I didn't do justice to where Harry, with everything gone wrong, is committing suicide from Westminster Bridge (zeroing his watch against Big Ben, the master mind to the end). As he is drowning a bottle floats by with a message in it. It reads, CLOSE SHOT: *"Dear Harry. . . ."*

And we get the chartered flying boat and the happy ending and the fortune teller in the fade-out scene (who turns out to be a celebrity actor) giving Harry and Orchard the date of the wedding.

"My God this is marvellous, Horace!" Arturo said. Then I heard him say: "Have you got that, Popsie?"

They get your stories whether you say yes or no. He would have the title registered by the time I saw him. This was to safeguard both of us. I trusted him implicitly. Besides *The Virgin Prostitute* was only the same old thing said in a different way. You only have one thing to say; sometimes you say it better than others.


I met Arturo Conti in several different ways over different periods of my life. The Italian who helped to start the

British film industry, was imprisoned by the British for being an alien, torpedoed by the Germans and finally sunk by the machine he created.

I saw him first on a cinema screen, in the newsreel. Arturo Conti with some of the beauties of the Cannes Film Festival. I was an engineer going to pieces between the factory, night classes, washing napkins and writing all night. I hated the plump Italian in the white suit with the beautiful bikini girls on the sunlit beach.

"I used to be a bastard, Horace," Arturo informed me later. "I had every girl there was. Every girl I met I had. No matter what the hell I had studio girls I had office girls I had cleaners I had—my God I had girls, Horace! Not any more. Finished. I love my wife." This sadly, miserably, then again alight with joy: "By God I was the biggest bastard on God's earth!"

I knew this was true, he was not bragging. Albert might have qualified for this distinction except that he was too busy polishing his own image to really give the time to it. I knew before I met him that Arturo was perhaps the greatest womaniser in the film business and that means in any business. One or two big name stars you might think greater but this is only because they got the publicity.

The film star and international playboy only goes for beautiful women which means they only have ten per cent to work on. They miss the studio girls, office girls, waitresses, factory girls, shop girls, cleaners; they miss the cream. They miss the greatest joy of all, the respectable girl, the moral girl, the religious girl, the girl who doesn't dress for men but only to keep warm.

In womanising, this is the earth. It means long hours and hard work but when the chink appears what you have is a total sacrifice, something that will wreck or wreathe their whole life. Good or bad this gives sex a meaning.

"Women who show their tits and wiggle their arses are just stupid bitches with men's minds," Arturo used to say, summing it up.

The making of a picture brings people together in intimate relationship as no other industry does. In the strange floodlit isolation of the studio sets and on remote beaches of Conrad islands, actors, actresses, directors, electricians, carpenters, writers, producers, prop men, camera men, wardrobe girls, hairdressers all quarrel, love, hate, despise, respect or remain indifferent in a limbo land halfway between fact and fiction. Then another picture, another family of people, another island, another hate another love.

People in films are like orphans who have been hardened off, cured of heartbreak, by being adopted by too many strangers.

Eventually you are sitting in a trattoria in Soho and the faces passing are like old gravestones moving.

"What do you think of Arturo Conti?" somebody asked me.

"He is a womanising bastard," I said, promptly.

At that time I had not even met him let alone worked with him. This is the trap you fall into. The anecdotes about people in the business are such common currency that soon you are discussing in familiar terms people you have never met. The point is you forget that it was not you that was there.

"We had this big panic conference going," the man said, "somebody had withdrawn the end-money two days after we started shooting. Flap? God! There was Alec Guinness, Cary Grant, Marilyn Monroe, you know—" He meant there was nobody I would know by name. "In comes this plain little girl to clean the telephone for God's sake. Arturo Conti clears the meeting. 'Give me five minutes,' he says. We all go out and place bets. Believe me, no word of a lie, in that five minutes he had had her on the desk!"

This I heard about Arturo before I met him. The next thing was a time when I was doctoring a script for a quick ten pounds and an additional-dialogue credit for a B-picture man and he one day beckoned me out of his crummy little office and along a corridor.

"This is what I'm going to have!" he said, opening a door.

It was a Hollywood film set of a film tycoon's luxurious office. It had everything except a bathing pool. An enormous crescent desk raised on a carpeted dais, gold furniture, deep blue drapes, oil masterpieces on tapestried walls, leather-panelled doors, the smell of cigars, six telephones, a private cinema annexe, a circular silk-covered bed with a bronze nude rising at the axle in a goat's embrace.

"Arturo Conti!" the B-picture man whispered.

He tried himself at the desk and then we crept out and back to the junk room he was renting.

Much later I was accused of stealing a story for a musical film I had written. The accusation and the injunction to stop the film exhibiting was made at the most profitable moment just as it was going on pre-release in a West-End art cinema. I don't know what happened although I was there. I often know what happens when I'm not there but when I am there I'm at a disadvantage. The mystique of the film business baffles me. Put simply, I don't know what anybody's talking about.

In front of the principals for both parties and two lawyers I had to swear that the story was original. This was easy because it was original. Everybody accepted my word, there was a lot of laughing and back-slapping and the man making the accusation was given ten thousand pounds. It was Arturo Conti.

"Nice work," he croaked to me, inexplicably, shaking my hand and almost kissing me. We had met at last under what he afterwards described as fortunate circumstances.

"I was so f—— skint!" he said.

He used the four-letter word for everything except the four-letter activity. To describe this he would avoid the word in a self-consciously gentlemanly way or else bash his fist against his arm as though doing it. At first shocked by this sexual mime, you later came to understand that in Italy it is quite delicate.

"One day," he said while we were all having a celebrating

drink together afterwards, "instead of stealing my stories you must come and write one for me."

I never discovered who was celebrating what. Everybody seemed quite happy that the picture had had an injunction slapped on it. There was a self-congratulatory air as though it proved we were A-picture people and in the big league.

It was like I'm sure the film which had its end-money stopped after two days of shooting. Like stars walking out in the middle of a picture and getting sued for a million pounds. You wait for a bankruptcy or a shot but no, there they still are, smiling, drinking, loving each other.

It's like kids playing cricket, they must use all the wickets to prove they're professional. As for the vast sums of money bandied about, I don't think anybody ever actually sees it in pennies and shillings and pound notes.

"What's this two hundred and forty pounds milk bill?" my bank manager asked me one day.

I couldn't explain it to him. What had happened was that while waiting for a distribution agreement for the picture that afterwards had a Royal Première I had found Tres unconscious in the gas-filled kitchen. I had had to break down the door and drag her out into the garden. Dramatising this to Arturo later that same day he had responded by asking me for a book.

"What sort of book?" I said.

"Don't f—— quibble," he said.

I gave him one of my Caxton Drakes in its ghastly penny-dreadful cover. He rushed round to somewhere and rushed back with a cheque for a thousand pounds made out to me.

"This is what you do," he said.

What I did was pay the thousand pounds into my account and then write cheques to various people for him. One to a milk firm—he had an ice-cream factory—one for Popsie, his secretary, one for his first wife and another to Doctor Barnardo's Home.

I was left with about two hundred pounds, which was unexpected and useful. What happened to the book God knows, or whether I ever signed away the film rights. I worked with him for two years and signed on average about six documents a day.

"Do you know you sold a documentary film company to an Italian combine?" Arturo's accountant asked me when they were clearing up the mess after his death.

I didn't know I ever had a documentary film company.

Distribution deals, participation deals, blanket deals, package deals, injunctions, re-sales, negative negotiations used to fly over my head in that Hollywood film set office while I was trying to explain some simple brilliant bit of dialogue that didn't seem to connect always with the Italian mind nor have much to do with what was going on at all.

"You see that wall?" Arturo would say. It was lined with stories and scripts that had never reached the screen. "One million pounds and ten years of my life. This one? *Hearts and Fury*. This one? *Beginner's Luck*. This one? Ah, shit. This is what they do to you, Horace. It is going through, it is not going through. Next Thursday, next Tuesday, next board meeting—look, you see this? Everything ready to shoot I give them—look, pages and f—— pages. Breakdown, budget, schedule, cross-plot, even the casting I do. Timing? I time right down to the last second—I show you. Popsie! She been with me thirty years. Too long. Popsie! Where is that bloody woman. Popsie! She is a cow, you know. She hears, she won't come. POPSIE! Horses you put out to grass. Ah, Popsie, hallo darling—where is timing? Here, tell Horace. Every f—— scene timed. All the figures. All we had to do was shoot. All right, go away. Seventy per cent the money I got. Seventy per cent the money! Still is not enough. They want all the bloody profits and put up nothing! My last picture a flop, the one before the biggest money spinner they ever have—they still running Rolls Royces on my picture before last! Now, nothing. Next Thursday. Perhaps. Your wife gasses herself? You know

they had my wife inside two days pumping her f——
stomach out! Next board meeting, next this, next that. We
should die they don't give a bugger. Those bastards, they
squeeze you and squeeze you. You know what they want
to give me on this? Fifty per cent! Forty per cent even!
They got the studios, they got the distribution, they got the
exhibition—what can I do? Buy cinemas? They got you
buggered Horace."

The telephone rings and Arturo draws himself into an
arrogant statue.

"You know who this is? That titled bastard—" his eyes
narrow "—I play it my way! 'ello? 'ello? My God!" A
stream of Italian lasting ten minutes and then, exhausted,
washed out, drooping across the crescent desk. "You are
up to your eyes, Horace? I am over my head!" He raises
his hands above his head and laughs loudly at this excruci-
ating joke. "My milk bill—one hundred forty pounds a
week!"

The ice-cream factory was steadily losing money, run
by Italian friends and relatives and boys from Rome he
had promised to do something for. They filtered in and
screamed across our script conferences.

"A sweet man but no f—— brains," Arturo would say
as they went out.

I would spend ten pounds a day travelling to and from
his office to hear about his life, his ruined stomach, his
relations, his war on the company who had him by the
short hairs and whose executives he lunched with every
day, taking them yet another revised version of our script
and coming back exuberant or deflated or furiously angry.

"You are professional, Horace? How many films? How
many books? Short stories? How many years? I am professional? I am making pictures when they suck their
mother's tits. Really bad pictures. Did I tell you? I had to
make bad pictures for the American company to make up
the British quota at ten thousand pounds each. There was
no script for Christ's sake. We made it up in front of the

cameras! I made I don't know how many—how many Popsie? Popsie! Where is that f—— woman? Never mind. You know what they do? I have just had lunch—you see me—that titled bastard. You know what he does? Every morning. He take a five pound note off the shelf and tucks it in his top pocket. Every night he put it back. Never spend a penny. Every day wining, dining, f—— at somebody else's expense! Five pounds in his pocket untouched! *This is his only aim in life!* Two million three hundred thousand pounds he got. I give him the script. Five copies Popsie stencilled—you saw. Everything, the breakdown, budget, blah blah blah—how long we work? Huh? Two months this time? Your wife suicide, my wife suicide, Popsie kicked out her flat? Two professionals, you and me, Horace. I know it's good, you know it's good, I got sixty per cent the budget, two hundred thousand pounds, they risk nothing —what he does? What he f—— does?" He screamed: "He give the f—— thing to his f—— typist—she's turned it down! She's turned the f—— thing down!"

Then a studio slot came up and the right four people hated the script (there was always this complicated board-room in-fighting) and a play fell through in New York making a star hard-up and the picture creaked on to the floor for Take One. It made a night's work for the guards' band, put another notch in Arturo's ulcer and bought Rolls Royces all round for somebody. There was a picture in the papers of some bronzed personality receiving royal con-gratulations on a fine achievement.

I didn't even know who he was.

Now thanks to Fiona Arturo Conti rode again. It could only be a re-make. The plot had to be the same.

# 10

# Arturo Conti

ARTURO CONTI strutted up Wardour Street as though he were in front of a band.

The place hadn't changed much since the days when I seemed to live there. The few new buildings and shop fronts had failed to make Soho look anything less like a sleazy fairground. The prevailing smell was still fried onions, the pavements still crowded with colourful natives busy with routine occupations and colourless provincials waiting for murder. The one difference was that the street prostitutes had been replaced—rather neatly I thought—by parking meters.

As frightened of sin and violence and foreigners, particularly foreigners, as the next country boy, Soho had at first terrified me; I walked around holding my pockets and waiting for a needle jab. Now I was tuned in to its sinister heart. It is not a law-abiding community but it obeys the more human canons of a gun-law town where a smile has more value.

We were on our way to the jousting. Arturo's demeanour was silent and grim. His other demeanour was insanely volatile. He would explode out on to the crowded lunch-time pavement of Wardour Street and accost the first beautiful girl he saw.

"You are very beautiful! You will get married and have many beautiful babies—or perhaps lovers. Go with my blessing!"

They didn't object. They never objected. They laughed, they blushed, but never frowned or looked frightened or embarrassed. I attempted this approach once while drunk and she walked on as if I hadn't spoken. You had to be Arturo. He would stare after her, punch me, croak as if talking through porridge:

"My God she is lovely! No? Do you want her, Horace? You bastard you want her! Once I was a bastard like you. Worse than you, Horace. Everything I did—" he would slam his fist against his elbow several obscene times "—typists, extras, stars, costume women, canteen girls! On the desk, the floor, the chair—you know how to do it in your car? Kneeling down—" he would kneel down on the pavement "—like this! You are just the right level." People in Wardour Street would smile and wave at these demonstrations. "My greatest friend, a famous gynaecologist, you know what he did? Every woman who came—they have this special chair for examination, you know? Just the right level." More arm slapping and then: " 'Why do you do this?' I ask him, 'every one?' He says: 'It is a compulsion! I have to do it, Arturo!' His wife understood this. They were very happy."

This was not today. Today he strutted, his face closed, his eyes steely. In this mood he would barely acknowledge—indeed completely ignore—the people we met and passed while they in turn seemed to become sober and silent as if the sun had gone in for a time, but understandably. He stopped by a tramp who always sat in the same passage on a pile of sacks and held a low-pitched furtive conversation with him. He would mutter in this way to the most unlikely people. In this mood I sometimes got the impression that he was the king-pin of a political conspiracy. That all these foreigners in Soho were waiting for the balloon to go up and when it did the signal would come from nobody but Arturo.

But all this secrecy and mood and tension resolved itself with a simple explanation on the doorstep of the restaurant,

[113]

a kind of film world's Atheneum, where he hissed to me with barely contained ecstasy: "I am lunching with that titled f——. You see. Sit inside the door. You watch. I make him take that fiver out his pocket." And a suppressed scream: "I left my wallet! I left my f—— wallet! My God —he will die! He will die!"

I watched. I listened. I sat inside the door with my pockets full of threepenny pieces I had taken from the children's money box to see me through the day. I heard them laughing and talking and loving each other, tasting from each other's forks, remembering old movies, old locations, old times. Arturo got to the torpedoing.

"I see this fellow standing on the rail beside me and as he jumps the life-jacket flap out in the wind. I say to myself 'That will break his neck!' It broke his neck as he hit the water. What I do? I jump holding mine like this with both hands. Six hours in the water in the dark. Holding on the same bit of wood a young chap with the top of his head off and screaming. We all shouting: 'Heil Hitler! Heil Hitler! Heil Hitler!' But the submarine goes. The only thing I get is my face trodden on when I climb the ladder to the ship."

Nothing about my story. Nothing about money. More about coming out of internment to find his film company, all his assets, gone.

"And my great friend—that shit!"

There were four of them by this time and they all looked round at me.

"Not him—you know Horace, a brilliant writer with more troubles than all of us. That other shit!"

A man lunching alone at the next table looked up and waved his fork.

"He come out a millionaire from giving people bad food in the war," Arturo informs the restaurant. "You see his new skyscraper out there? 'How you get all this?' I ask him. He is another f—— millionaire! 'Arturo,' he says, 'I am lucky.' He is lucky! He is a crook is the secret! 'Arturo,' he say, 'before I am interned I have this one café losing money. When I come out very fortunately they are bombing London to hell and everybody wants cups of tea on the street!' True or false?"

The man at the next table nodded its truth with a smiling mouthful of food.

"Soon he will be another titled bugger like you," Arturo said to his friend.

They were all laughing together as I came out.


Because I was not thinking I went up in Arturo's cabbagy lift. I remembered before I got to the top and burst out into his suite, afraid the door would be locked. I am terrified of lifts. Freda the telephonist looked up from a book. She was a big nice Chinese girl with a perspiration problem. I unloaded my threepenny bits on to her desk.

"Again?" she said. "You don't change."

"So let's make love," I said.

"Is there still time?"

"Lock the lift door," I said, "again."

We used the circular silk bed in the Hollywood office. Funny, I could do it with her. I wasn't mad about her or in love with her or any of those inhibitions.

"Buon giorno!" a litle voice said.

A tiny pretty Italian girl stood there, about three years old, an Italian comic in her hand.

"Oh Chlist," Freda said. "I florglot."

"Is papa coming now?" the little girl said.

We dressed, sat the little girl at her father's desk, unlocked the lift doors, put the kettle on for tea, got the change for the threepenny bits organised.


I was half-sleeping, relaxed, on the bed when I heard Arturo Conti and his young wife come into the outer office.

[115]

"I am expecting a call from Rome."

"You've had it, Mr Conti. An hour ago."

"Get back to them. . . ."

Lorraine came in with the child. She had left her with Freda while she went in search of her husband.

"Hello, Horace." She kissed me on the cheek. "Don't let him work too late."

She told me these things quickly. I was not to accept any great promises from Arturo. He was a sick man. He would never direct another picture. He should settle for a production contract. He could produce three pictures while somebody younger directed them.

"While he insists on directing they'll keep him out altogether," she said. "Suggest it to him. We're all trying to suggest it to him." And: "What have you got in your garden?" she went on, as Arturo came in.

"Out!" Arturo told his family.

"Bring Horace home to dinner," Lorraine said.

"Horace is going to Rome," Arturo Conti said.

Lorraine flashed me a warning look as she went out.

"Your wife telephoned," Arturo told me then.

"My wife did? Which one? When? What about?"

"Lie down, Horace. I'm worried about your wife. You've got your flies undone."

He lay flat on the circular bed, his eyes closed. He fumbled at loosening his tie, unbuttoning his coat, kicked his shoes off. I lay down forty-five degrees away. I heard the lift doors open, the little bilingual child chattering as they went.

"What you been doing all this time? Why don't you come to see me if you are in trouble? You know your trouble, Horace? You only go to see people about work. You got no friends. Friends is a waste of time. I have got so many friends. You must have friends. Your wife will commit suicide. She say she have no money, no food, no sweets, no piano lessons."

It was Fiona.

[116]

He was only now struck by this odd kind of starvation:
"She will go mad!"

Arturo was the only person in the film business Tres had
liked. I took her up to lunch with him the day after his
baby was born. She had sat there in her old-fashioned
clothes, the straw hat, the Calliope Jane make-up, stunned
by the language but touched at Arturo's intoxicated behaviour around the restaurant about the baby. He was so
jubilant he had done it again at fifty-nine was one of the
reasons.

I knew now that the story had nothing to do with my
being there.

"What did they think of the story?" I asked.

"What story?" he said. "Oh, that one. That bitch has
not typed it up yet. You know where she is? Having her
hair done! It is time she was going to the embalmers. I
tell her: 'I am going to have you stuffed and put you up
on top of this f—— bed.'" He rattled a laugh and expired
again. He regained some breath. "Lorraine say I swear
too much. You think I swear too much? It is this bloody
business."

Freda came in and put two cups of tea on the side table,
took her panties from under the cushion, touched me up
in passing as she went out.

"She is sweating today," Arturo remarked. "Tell me
something, Horace. Do you ever have her? Oh, I forget, you
don't talk about it. You write about it for ten million
people to read but you don't talk about it. You know what?
That titled bastard won't open his f—— mouth if there
is a writer present. How much do you need a week, Horace?
Fifty pounds? One hundred? You have the office next door
to me. Get in what time you like, go when you like, bring
your girls in—I get a bed fixed. What you say? I tell you
why. This f—— business is no good. You know what I
am doing? The biggest script agency in the world. Films,
television, every bloody thing. Before long you are clearing
a thousand a week and a share of the profits. I make you

[117]

a director, Horace. What the hell, you won't do it."

There was no answer required for this kind of rhetoric. I shied away from being harnessed as from nothing else. Not even for the headmaster's wife's corsets would I do it.

"You are so touchy about your work but soft as shit about everything else." Arturo told me, his chest still heaving, his eyes still tightly closed. "That is how it should be. I make only the films I want to make. No crap for me. A man has to take a stand if it kills him. Me, I am already dead, Horace."

The slaughter on the roads has nothing on the slaughter in the film business. When the end-product is comedy the casualties increase. At best you are in a tomb, planning resurrection.

"Also I want you to write my story," Arturo wheezed as if they were his last words.

This depressed me, like coming in at the funeral instead of the wedding by mistake.

"Why don't you take your subject to another company?" I asked him.

I wanted like hell to see him on the floor again, calling for action, making his obscene jokes, cuddling the leading lady and showing her how it should be done.

"I let you into a secret, Horace," Arturo said. "Everything I put up I send copies to all the majors. No bloody good. You know why? They got an agreement with each other: *Bugger Arturo Conti.*"

The call came from Rome. Arturo opened his eyes at Freda's yell and took hold of the world again. He sprang up, went across to the big crescent desk with his shoes in one hand, the tea in the other. He took some tablets with his tea as he talked in Italian, using all the wickets. He clicked his fingers at me as he listened to the other part. I gave him a cheque book and a pen. He wrote a bearer cheque for two hundred pounds and uncrossed it, gave it to me.

"This is what you do, Horace," he said, when the call

was finished. "You would like to go to Rome tomorrow?"

Freda came in, precise and dainty on small feet the way fat people do. "Mr Al Dalgleish."

"Come in, come in Al," Arturo shouted. "Don't go," he told me as I moved politely. "You know Al? He used to be a top gangster. You know where the Chicago gangsters went after prohibition ended? Hollywood. They spent the next twenty years filming their memoirs. This is what we are fighting—how are you you old bastard?" This latter to the American as they clasped and hugged each other.

"The deal has gone through, Arturo," Al Dalgleish said.

"Good," Arturo said. "I got the money." And about me: "This is Horace Spurgeon Fenton—a brilliant writer."

"Of course! Of course!" Al Dalgleish said. "My God I like your stuff." He mentioned the football story by the other Fenton and went on: "And they say the flashback is old-hat—boy, it was brilliant! You know what I think about the old movie tricks? You know what I think, Arturo. You can't top 'em. 'Cos why?" He shared the message between both of us but more towards me as if Arturo already knew that he was well-known for this message. "Those boys who discovered the motion picture camera invented every trick that we know today. They had surrealism and all we did was take it into the corn belt. The camera is the box that can make dreams come true. Not plays come true, not stories come true but dreams come true, every fantastic thing come true from imaginings from urges from wishes from memories from impressions from everything in the human condition—you know *Marienbad*? René Clair's *Entr'acte* in nineteen-twenty-four for God's sake!" And rationally and quietly to Arturo as if his lecture to me was to another camera: "You ever play cards?"

"Picture cards with my little girl. You know I got a little girl? Three years old! Everything she say in two languages. My God—you know? Sometimes—she is so bright, so intelligent, so shrewd, such an actress—I tell you I am frightened!"

"That's good," Al Dalgleish said, mildly. "You go round to the Savoy and play cards with the big man himself—you lose five thousand pounds. Okay?"

"Okay," Arturo Conti said, automatically, then, "play cards? Why don't I just give him the money?"

"You got to lose it at cards, Arturo. It's the way he does it. Shit, what do you care? You get your deal—quarter million guarantee no questions, no script approval, no cast approval—look, I'll get you slotted in for—how much location have you got?"

"Three weeks two days, five nights work—one unit half the time, two units for five days, a crane I want three, maybe four shots is all and a crowd of fifty for two nights and then three nights the stars and seven nights on doubles with—just a minute, I got it here, everything, budget, breakdown, cross-plot, where is it—Popsie! Where is that f—— woman—never mind she is out—" He stopped rummaging and looked up as if he had encountered something new for the first time in film business: "I don't understand these cards, Al?" It was a wicket he had not used yet.

"I'll put it in synopsis," Al Dalgleish said. "Rock's having his throat cut for alimony by his last ex and has to prove he is skint so contacts the bank and Christ—he *is* skint. Uncle Sam, you know, the last lousy movie, Castro, Vietnam, five wives so anyway he makes his next big production under a phoney name and that's tied up and he's over here and needs cash to operate for three say four weeks— that's fifteen thousand dollars in round. That's your five thousand, Arturo, now read on. Studios? I can slot you in at Pinewood—two stages free October—Elstree, several possibilities or maybe Dublin, plenty of facilities at Ardmore now and cheaper—"

"Not cheaper any more, Al. Sure, the prices are lower maybe but going up, you got to take the units there, cast, all expenses, against what? Even extradition they got now.

You can't offer the boys sanctuary from wives, debts, rape any more—I stick to my own connections. I give them the picture, the rental, U.K. distribution—they give me a better deal." He said this gloomily and without conviction as though it were not so much a probability as just symmetrical. "I still don't understand about the cards, Al," he added. "What's the difference I put it into his hand?"

"You pass money at cards there's no come-back. From the government for instance—was it a gift was it a loan was it an investment? No blackmail either—not that you would—"

"Oh my God now I understand. I myself am being blackmailed at this moment—two thousand pounds! Some bloody woman. Six, seven years ago. She said it was a loan —it was an investment, the picture was never made. You see my walls? All pictures never made. Two thousand pounds and pay her boy's school fees—Eton she sends him to! I swear I don't even know he is mine!"

"Well now you see. You should have just played her cards, Arturo. You know what Daisy's done to Rock? That place in Los Angeles he had—that palace? She got the lot and she's started herself the biggest TV casting agency on the coast. She's representing all her ex-husbands. Can you imagine ten per cent of an oil well? Multiply that by seven, you've got an oil well except for the top three feet and that she's working on."

"How is she?"

"How do you think?"

"Beautiful woman, Daisy. Such movement!" Arturo said. And to me: "You should meet her, Horace. You know something? When she was over here supposed to be in Paris choosing her trousseau—ah, never mind."

"Snap!" Al Dalgleish said. "But why they have to marry them!"

"It is religion," Arturo explained, soberly. "They are Catholic, like me. Very strict. That is a very good trick about the cards. Do you mind if I make a note. . . ."

The American stopped Arturo scribbling, tore off the page of his desk diary and screwed it up.

"I am sorry," Arturo said.

"Is he safe?" Al now said about me. "He hasn't said a word since I came in. I don't trust writers. They hang around listening to everything, sit there shifty-eyed, mouthing the dialogue to themselves, working out how the construction will be, getting the payoffs—" and with mock praying: "Please, Horace!"

I crossed my heart but too low down.

"Now what about the casting?" Al Dalgleish said.

"The casting I got," Arturo said, delving into papers.

"Never mind the men," Al Dalgleish said, "who's playing Jane?"

Arturo mentioned a star who was reading it.

"Ah-ah," said Al Dalgleish. "Never mind the character. It has to be a new bit of arse." And to me: "Else what's in motion pictures? Let's have the short list and boy is it short."

They started browsing through *Spotlight* as though looking for somewhere to live. For half the beautiful innocent faces in the book they had foul anecdotes.

"You know something?" Arturo said. "Instead of losing I am going to win. I am so unlucky this time I am going to win!"

"Nuts. You just go to the john and leave your cards on the table that's all you have to do. When you come back you'll lose, I promise you."

At times like this I was thankful that I was not a part of the film industry. Writers are always somewhat on the outside. Because of this perhaps, only half-understanding the business or what's being said, they get the feeling that they are caught up in something crooked. The writer who writes about crime, murder, immorality, human frailty, has a built-in fear that any of these things should touch his non-writing life. Yet oddly, as a good script editor once told me (he lent me money, passed my scripts without touching a word, got the sack) the criminal mind is strangely akin to the writer's mind—meaning artists, actors, the whole fiction world.

"You'll find that if you are sober you suck up to the police," he said one day as we walked down Kingsway, "and if you are drunk you try to hit them."

We have the habitual criminal's self-deception, self-aggrandisement, evasiveness and the art of charming and conning and not facing facts. The man therefore who finds himself completely a criminal except that he has not broken the law goes around in perpetual fear of putting a foot wrong.

"It will have to be cash," Al Dalgleish said. "No cheques, nothing you can record or trace."

"Five thousand pounds in new fivers," Arturo was promising now.

"Fine, good, great." Al Dalgleish said. "Hey look at this? What about this?" They had come to another beautiful halfway famous face.

"She's in a play," Arturo said. "In New York. She won't be through till December." He talked as if he was in close touch with every girl in that three-thousand-page book.

"So we wait till December?" Al Dalgleish said.

"I must get locations in by October latest for the weather —otherwise we shoot them South of France that means twenty-five thousand pounds extra charges per week. *Per week!*" You'd never catch him without the figures.

"And, what's most important?" Al Dalgleish said, holding up the picture.

"You f—— her you f—— the picture," Arturo promised.

"You want me to come in tomorrow?" I suggested.

They became aware that I was there again.

"This is the part he don't like," Arturo explained.

"Are you queer?" Al Dalgleish asked me, as one would say "Do you like smoked salmon?"

"Not yet," I said.

"I give him actresses—how many actresses I give you,

[123]

Horace? Ten? Twenty? They say to me—he takes them to the pictures!—they say 'He is very gentlemanly.'"

"I don't know how to break the ice with them," I said.

"What ice!" Dalgleish said, incredulously.

"And yet you know—" Arturo dropped his voice, clicked his fingers towards the outer office: "Freda? Very nice girl but—you know." And he banged his fist against his arm.

The American made a comic pretence of psycho-analysing me and then got back to *Spotlight*.

"This one for sure!"

"She's dead."

"And never called me mother—" the glossy pages flipped "—how about this?"

"In Hollywood," Arturo said.

"This?"

It was June Chappell, The Countess.

"I've had that," I said.

Funny, when they said things like that it sounded smooth and not too bad. When I said it it embarrassed them and then me. Why is that? Sometimes I have—when for instance I see somebody I know coming or I'm going into a shop—sometimes I have to rehearse with myself saying "Good morning" or "Nice day" or "What weather again!" I have to rehearse it. Anything everybody else says that I feel I ought to say sometimes to sound normal. My God, now I've got it down I see it. *I am trying to be normal!*

"That bitch! My God what an actress! You know something? I had her straight out of drama school. You know what part I gave her? A bus conductress! Her next film —whooomph! But not for me. I am a cunt." Then, remembering who he was talking to and the deal, he promised: "Not any more."

"I met her in Hollywood," Al Dalgleish said, about another face. "She brought her mother."

"The mothers are the best," Arturo assured him. "Especially English mothers. I tell you, the mothers I have had

[124]

in Rome. All their lives screwed through a wedding ring in Hampstead and now—boom!"

"Age shall not weary them nor the years condemn," the American said.

I started laughing and I couldn't stop. I can never compete with this kind of talk. You want to hate them but you can't.

"Good, huh?" Al Dalgleish said, genuinely flattered as though he respected my judgment.

"I tell him," Arturo said, "he must write my story. You know who would play my part?"

"Di Sica?" Dalgleish hazarded.

"No no. He is a good friend of mine but no. Too much—" he indicated weight, bearing "—like a bank manager. No— Alberto Sordi. Brilliant. *Now* he is a maniac! *Now* he is f——!"

"Self-knowledge is a great thing," Al Dalgleish said, glancing at me for reaction.

I couldn't honestly laugh at that and he lost interest in me.

"This five thousand, Arturo? No strings, eh? It's not entailed in any way? We don't want any claims. I don't exactly want to know where you're getting it from, but you know?"

"It is an unconditional loan from a great friend in Rome. I was talking to him just before you come in. Is that right, Horace? It is all ready. No letters, no receipts, no forms, no customs worries. Horace is flying over tomorrow to pick it up in a plain black bag and bring it straight back to me."

I felt ill.

# 11

# Paris

I WENT TO PARIS WITH A NUN. I happened to get in the same
carriage of the boat train at Victoria. I happened to see her
as I was coming through the booking hall—the international booking hall is across that little road, you remember—and she was getting out of a taxi with a small girl
and I happened to follow them to the Golden Arrow
and run like mad the last fifty yards to open a door for
her.

She was young but not very pretty; pale, as though she
had been under a stone but not worm-eaten the way some
of them are, as if they've tried everything else first. She
was very much alive and excited as if this trip was a hell
of a thing for her. Even me she treated as though I'd happened rather than just met her. She gave me some crusty
bread to eat and some garlicky kind of sausage meat and
let me drink out of her flask of milk.

To get on the train to Paris I had started off at London
Airport if you can work that out.

"You can't get out now!" the air hostess practically
screamed at me when I dragged my holdall to the door of
the Viscount.

"I've got claustrophobia," I told her.

They had to radio control, get the steps back, open the
doors—it took fifteen minutes to get out. That alone justi-
fies anybody's claustrophobia. All the passengers were

wearing pitying frozen smiles of sheer panic by the time I got off. They thought I'd had some sort of premonition. I don't know what kind of trip they had.

I crept into Arturo Conti's office during lunch time while there was nobody around dragging my heavy bag. Instead of being out at lunch he was sitting at his big crescent desk playing cards with himself; he jumped, guilty as hell. I forget the exact date, but try to remember that this is what independent film production had come to in this country: *he was practising losing*.

"Thank God!" he croaked when he saw me. He jumped up and clasped me in his arms. "You know what I thought? I thought you would be in prison! I tell Al after you are gone 'He will finish up rotting in some bloody Italian prison!' I tell you something? He agreed with me!" He was laughing hysterically now. "That bastard! He would let you do it! 'He'll never smuggle five thousand pounds from Italy,' he say. 'He could not smuggle his own shit,' he say. 'Everything that man has got is written in his face— that bloody face is right out of an ash-can,' he say." He shook my hand. "You have save me, Horace. I love you like a son." He went down on his knees and started opening my holdall.

I let him. I let him. They had both stated categorically that I would not be breaking the law. They told me this for a whole hour because for a whole hour I had told them that I would. Don't tell me it's legal to bring currency from one country into another. If it is, then I've given away a lot of money in my time, sending people on holiday to Spain and Jugoslavia to spend royalties I couldn't get any other way and not being able to afford the fare or the time to go myself.

"My God!" Arturo said, when he couldn't find the money.

He turned as grey as an army blanket when I told him I hadn't been yet. He had this knack of turning grey and collapsing into his chair as though you had just shot him in the back. He would do it if I got there on Friday and he'd been waiting since Monday for a script conference; or if he was waiting for a vital synopsis and I came out of the back office with an essay which I had just happened to feel like writing instead.

"You will be too late," he said, when I finally agreed to go to Rome by train.

You always got a split-second time element coming into this stage of setting up a picture where if you don't have the re-write on the great man's desk by ten o'clock in the morning sharp then the whole half-million pound picture is shot and they're going ahead with another subject. And the great man after you've collapsed into his office with three copies bungs them across to his typist who browses through them when she's finished this month's Crozzle in *She*.

"I don't like the man," she says at last (he is eighty per cent).

And this isolated executive who lives between his Rolls Royce his office and the boardroom plays safe and does another re-make of *The Thirty-Nine Steps*. One typist whose favourite programme is *Peyton Place* and he thinks he's got his finger on the public pulse. The horrifying thing is he has.

Arturo Conti was right—I was too late. He died. I killed him along with all the other scriptwriters; they killed him along with all the other big film companies; you killed him along with all the other people who stay away from cinemas these days.

But it was Albert, my milkman, who pressed the button.

### ARTURO CONTI FOUND DEAD

The first thing I do arriving at a foreign town is go for a London paper and this headline was waiting for me at the *Gare du Nord* in Paris. Not you notice *Film Producer Found Dead* but *Arturo Conti Found Dead*. This is the subtle distinction we are all slaving our guts out for. This is the title we all want.

"He was your uncle?" the nun asked, gently.

"Yes," I said.

I was lying.

The child stared at me as she had been staring at me all the way from Victoria to Dover, from Dover to Dunkirk, from Dunkirk to Paris. I should think she was about nine, with misleading pigtails and the kind of cynical dead-pan expression which some children have.

With the young nun herself I had made hay. I had had plenty of time after all. I had eaten her bread, drunk her milk, discussed various religious theses with her and for a breathless few minutes going through northern France I had had her sleeping head resting against my shoulder. I tried to get my knee against her leg but caught the child looking at me under her deceitful lashes.

I had learned that she was called Sister Olivia and that she was taking the child from a convent school in Edinburgh to her parents in Paris. I gathered that she belonged to an ancient and pretty rugged order and was not one of these hot-head nuns you see flashing around Hammersmith in punchy cars at all hours.

She learned about me that I wrote semi-religious books.

"And are you going to write a script about Rome?" she asked me.

"If I was I would go to Wigan," I told her. I mean it. Writers who manage to go to the North Pole and the Congo to get their material I greatly admire. All you need to do is breathe in and out.

"I'll get you a taxi," I offered while we were still around the bookstall on the station. "It occurred to me," I said (it is difficult to phrase your words when you know a nine-year-old girl is way ahead of you) "that you might like me to show you around Paris for a few hours. After you've delivered your charge?" I don't really talk like that.

"That's very kind of you, Spurgeon," she said.

"Oh my God!" the little girl said (I saw her lips move). She looked to heaven in exasperation and did a very professional dry-wash of her little face with her little hand (the slow burn) as we got into the taxi.

She kept saying "love" I remembered as I sat outside some ugly Victorian barrack in one of the suburbs of Paris (someone should write a song about the suburbs of Paris). "That would be lovely" and "I'd love to" and several times "I love that". Was this an unconscious expression of what she really wanted all the time she was saying her Hail Mary's and De Profundis or sitting under the skull eating her gruel or doing her penance to the old M.S. for getting up late? Was it love that she really wanted all the time? (I know what I'd want.)

"Mr Fenton?"

Papa stood there with the taxi door open. I knew it was Papa—Mama was at the open front door with the child, several other people including a gendarme were grouped about the doorstep. No sign of Sister Olivia.

I never saw her again although I always keep a sharp eye on nuns. What I imagine had happened was that while Mama had been shaking hands with Sister Olivia the child had been swiftly briefing her old man about the bum outside.

He regretted that Sister Olivia had decided to stay—no, he didn't, he didn't. You see you can over-type when you're rushed like this with one ear on the door. He didn't mention Sister Olivia which made it more of an insult I remember. Our arrangement and the reason I was sitting there was completely ignored. He thanked me for being so helpful to his daughter and her "guardian" on the journey and invited me for dinner.

I said something about having an urgent appointment at the Darryl Zanuck office (I only name-drop when I'm fighting back) and in almost the same breath shouted my driver to drive on.

With all those accusing eyes on me as we drove away I

never felt so mean, small, dirty—unclean is a better word—
lecherous, foul; so transparent you could read small print
through me.

"The great thing about your lemonade personality is
your absinthe face," old Angie once told me. She had a
sharp line in epigrams and wit. About poppies in a corn-
field we were riding through she said: "They're beautiful.
They're like orgasms." I was wishing for her a bit as I sat
in a bar along by the river.

The drug of the month was coming out of a juke box
and I liked it. I felt that I was in Paris and not in Welwyn
Garden City. Sad and glad and a bit adventurous.

*Guess there's no use in hanging round.*
*Guess I'll get dressed and do the town. . . .*

I worried for the lyric writer about the two guesses and
then wondered if he had finally considered it poetically
better, the repetition.

Children were dancing in front of the music. Just twitch-
ing and watching each other with dirty minds. Because it
was obvious, it was clean. Better than the sidelong thought.

*I'll find some crowded avenue.*
*Though it will be empty without you. . . .*

I thought about Hemingway, Fitzgerald, Pound; that
I'd missed it again. That when it was the right time I was
only just starting on my stench-pole period. I put on my
dark glasses.

There are two things I do that are not quite genuine when
I'm in the kind of place where you might find some young
girls half-gone. One is put on dark glasses to hide my half-
century of creases and look a bit artistic; the other is, if I've
been found out, to scan the place casually through my
squared fingers as though I'm getting locale for a film. I
was doing this when the police moved in.

There was the traditional squeal of brakes and the rush
of uniformed bodies plus the plain-clothes man who has

been watching Maigret. I wasn't nervous or apprehensive at all this time because exactly the same thing had happened when I'd been sitting with Alice in a café in Caen. About a dozen policemen had rushed in and ordered Coca-Colas.

"You've turned as white as a sheet, Fenton!" Alice had said.

This time they rushed in and surrounded me. The detective asked me if my name was Fenton and I admitted it. It gave me asthma. I thought about my asthma spray and realised that it was in the holdall and I had left it in the taxi.

"I've lost my case," I told them, just as if I'd sent for them.

"We have it, M'sieu," the detective said.

"Well, that's very good of you," I told him.

I was terrified. I knew damn well they hadn't come to give me my case back. My first fear was that somebody had informed on Arturo about the money. But it wasn't that. They took me to the police station leaving somebody, I gathered, to watch the café. At the station I was identified by the taxi driver and then by who I thought was a total stranger but afterwards remembered as Papa. So it was about the nun, then. I didn't see what I'd done but then you never do in a foreign country.

By this time I had asthma so badly I could hardly breathe and they let me lie on a couch in the charge room. Lying down doesn't help asthma but they kept me like it until I'd seen a doctor who lifted up my eyelids with nicotined fingers and then nodded mysteriously to the detective. I recognised the scene. They thought I was pushing horse. Was an addict.

The detective, watching my face, then took a green baize cloth off the table and revealed the contents of my holdall all laid out like exhibits. It wasn't pretty. I used the case to empty my pockets into, carry my personal things between homes, I practically lived out of it. I hadn't bothered to empty it out for the trip but had just put a few extra things in. There were dirty handkerchiefs and used tissues (asthma is not a pretty complaint), socks with holes in, grubby shirts, mucky pants, half eaten apples gone brown, suggestive bits of chitterling; and everything laid out as if it was significant.

The detective examined my asthma inhaler as though it might go off in his hands. Then he carefully replaced it alongside my family-size packet of contraceptives and pessaries as though that is where it belonged. I knew what he was thinking. The inhaler is a large black plastic chamber with a nozzle one end and a rubber squeeze bulb the other. I got my face slapped once when I brought it out in a cinema. The funny thing is nobody really knows what they think it is.

I won't milk this episode for more than it's worth. The taxi driver had opened the case and found a note pinned on to one of my clean shirts. It was from Tres.

*Remember the eighteenth or you'll be arrested again—T.*

He had taken it to the police who interpreted it as a blackmail note. From this slender beginning they had decided that my asthma inhaler was for procuring abortions, my ephedrine tablets were heroin, that I was in the White Slave traffic—the little girl probably put in a word there—and that contraceptives were a sideline. They had staked out the café in the hope of clapping eyes on my Paris contact.

Several things stopped me answering this adequately straight away; the first that I couldn't breathe until they'd given me Exhibit A. Then the plain-clothes type held my passport in front of him and asked me my address; I guessed at it and got it wrong. I thought I'd be stuck then explaining about my two homes. This could take hours at home. Not in France, though.

"Naturally," he said.

Then while searching me they found one of my tunes written out on the back of one of Albert's visiting cards (I had pockets full of his visiting cards).

"What is this?" the detective asked.
It read:

FSFSA FSFFSA BBFBBBFBE BFBBFBBFBE CSBGEBDB

"It's a tune," I told him.
He turned the card over in that pointed manner they
have. On Albert's side in gold gothic it said:

ADAM'S PLAYGROUND
*Members only*
*Address: Keep it quiet!*
*Manager: Albert Harris*

*Service a speciality—Food incidental.*

He considered this would intrigue without arousing sus-
picion. He spent a lot of time and trouble and ran up a lot
of printer's bills for this kind of thing.

Charles Fenton got me out of most of my troubles. Somebody at the police station turned up a translation of his
football story. They were full of apologies.

"You should have mentioned the book first!" the detective said.

They didn't appear to have changed their minds about
me; it was just that if I was a writer, okay. The whole attitude to the arts is different over there. I got minor celebrity
treatment after that, though I noticed they kept the card
with my tune on it.

They gave me a dinner at the King George V and quite
a nice room. We had a party there. The detective and some
of his colleagues and some more people they turned up in
my honour; one or two journalists and publicity folk, some
bright girls including one who bent nails in her teeth in a
cabaret act. All drug addicts, by the look of them. Even
the police had black panda eyes. The French all look as if
they never go out.

The true purpose of the party didn't emerge until about

[134]

four o'clock in the morning when in came a shifty character who whispered to the detective who then came over to me and lifted off the nail-bending girl.

"What sort of tune?" he said, holding the card out for explanation.

They'd been trying all night to break the code and failed. I sang it to him. The music, if you want to pick it out, is:

*F sharp, F sharp, A – F sharp, F, F sharp, A – B, B flat, B, B, B flat, B, E – B flat B, B flat B, B, F, B E – C sharp, B, G, E bottom, D bottom.*

This in the key of D-major using the accompanying chords D, D-diminished, D, A7, Repeat, B minor, B flat minor, B minor, B flat minor, A7, D7, A7, D.

I sang:

> *"I'm eating toffees,*
> *In the office,*
> *I'm drawing you on my blotter,*
> *I know I didn't otter,*
> *Are you drawing me?"*

The party broke up quickly after that. They all seemed a bit tetchy as though they'd done a useless night's work. Except the cabaret girl who was high. I don't believe she was a cabaret girl, now I come to think of it.

Albert didn't like my tunes either, whether I made them up or not, and I can never stop whistling.

"What's that?" he would say.

"*Doing The Uptown Lowdown,*" I would tell him.

"Oh boy!" he would say.

He thought they dated me.


I had to fly back from Paris because it was Saturday and getting late. If I wasn't there to buy Edna a choc-ice in the front circle all the kids got on to me.

"If you're not here Saturday night," Sue would say, "everything comes home to her."

# 12

# The Catalytic Milkman

I GOT BACK TO HAWTHORN WAY too late for the pictures and found the house dark and empty. I wandered round through all the old rooms of my life feeling neglected, deserted, bereaved and frightened.

*Ladybird, ladybird, fly away home,*
*Your house is on fire and your children are gone.*

This invocation to a ladybird sitting on the back of my hand as a child always filled me with fear and dread and cold loneliness.

KEEP TOY CUPBOARD TIDY—NANA said a postcard drawing-pinned in the cupboard under the stairs when I put a shilling in the meter. The card had been there at least fifteen years since they were children and my mother the reigning guest in the house, looking after them and looking after Edna.

"She's like a child," my mother used to say. "You poor thing."

She wasn't perfect, either. She used to think that every-body was trying to starve her and creep down in the night and cut herself chunks of bread and jam, carefully remov-ing the crumbs afterwards. She died in June, 1957 (sold to *Argosy*).

The children came in and brought their chums, yobs and

floosies like us. I asked Sue where her mother was and she told me she'd waited until it was almost too late and had then accepted an offer from Mr Fortin and gone with him.

"Don't talk as though it hasn't happened before," Lang said. His mates laughed.

Sue said: "One more wife, Daddykins, and you'll be losing Mummykins. You wouldn't want that!"

"Why don't you get yourself sterilised, dad?" Lang suggested.

"You get *yourself* sterilised," I told him. "You'll feel differently about it once you start enjoying yourself."

"He's right, you know," Sue said, rubbing her nails on her other cuff.

One of their yobs cut in, earnestly: "It don't affect nuffink y'know Mr Fenton."

I don't know where they all get these mixed-up introverted teenagers from for our entertainment, not from anybody I've ever met. I got more artistic understanding and appreciation from the Berts and Freds and Russells and Sandras than from anybody in my own age group.

"Don't sit there showing your fat arse while Mr Fenton's trying to concentrate, Betty," they would say.

"Your old man's f—— brilliant," I heard one of them tell Lang one day.

They were perceptive not only about me but about the world, the cosmos, the human condition. This particular bosom pal of Lang's, Russ, I think it was, was a gravedigger in the evenings and weekends, a dustman by day; oddly related activities he had decided. "You fink abaht it," he said to me as somebody who would understand: "I clear up man's refuse all day and God's refuse in me spare time— right?" I know he didn't read it anywhere because he couldn't read.

"Do you mind if I use that?" I said.

He was so chuffed. It got so that they would do anything for me.

"Will you pop me home on your way?" Betty used to ask;

I forget whose friend she was but I know she was mine. "Can I ask you a personal question?" she asked me one night. And when I agreed she said: "Have you actually spoke to Frank Sinatra?" He was a popular singer and actor (this may be known to you but not to the man borrowing his book on the village green from the hovercraft which has just zoomed in, the nineteen-eighty-four man for whom I am also writing).

Frank Fortin and Edna came in together still laughing at the film.

"Whatever's the matter with you?" Edna said.

I was sitting down amongst the kids. I never sat down in either house. Not just to sit. I didn't have a chair. I was always moving, working, in transit, checking supplies, going somewhere or coming back. Because she was not there I had forgotten where I was; fallen into the habitual thing of sitting in a teenage haunt.

"Hope you didn't mind, Mr Fenton?" Frank Fortin said.

I did mind for about a dutiful ten seconds when I'd first been told. She was one of my gang after all. I can get possessive about an old boot. But this was outweighed by the off-loading relief. For one of my women to go out with another man was as unexpected and astonishing and welcome as one of Tres's cats going out and getting itself a job and making itself independent. I felt glad for her, too.

I used to go in sometimes late evenings and find her with all the lights out except the television, standing up in front of it. Or standing knitting in a corner. She was always alone. Once, worst of all, I heard her laughing at one of those inane linkage lines a disc jockey had just put across. I think it was the saddest thing I ever heard in my life.

They kicked Edna around for her stupidity but they looked after her because of it. She knew this and it warmed her; it made them all a part. They built their characters together and they built strongest where the bits were missing in their home life.

[138]

Frank Fortin stooped his grey head to murmur to me on the back doorstep when I saw him out that night. I thought he was going to say: "I'll tell you something about that dog."

"I wondered if you'd mind if I took Mrs Fenton to the hospital on Tuesday afternoon?"

I told him not at all.

"I want to get her ears looked at," he said.

I don't want to sound far-fetched but Tres was up when I got home that night. This was far more unnerving than finding nobody at Edna's.

"I want to talk to you," she said.

This was ridiculous. She didn't have a mood on—well yes she did have a mood on; kind, soft, placid, rational. She made me some cocoa.

"I've sold the house," she said then.

I'd been away what—two, three days. I should never have given her that money it was like kissing the sleeping beauty. She'd got operational. What I did was with that two hundred of Arturo's take out fifty and give seventy-five pounds each to Edna and Tres. Edna you would never know had it but Tres knew how to make money work. She could make a penny work.

She had got up at crack of dawn on the Friday, fed the animals, cleaned the ranch, fettled the bunkhouse, kept the kids away from school, hired a taxi for the whole day, done a tour of the range and fences; the bank, the estate agents, the psychiatric hospital, the shops.

"You haven't noticed anything, have you?" she said.

I did then, too late as usual. The main room had been repainted and decorated in cream and lavender, there were new green curtains, two white rugs, new floral loose covers on the three-piece and she was wearing a new dress. She had got it all done before the buyer came. She had been to the bank to squash the equity arrangement and arrange finance.

[139]

There would be enough money to get her and the children into a flat in London and she was going to work.

"I'm sick of the way you muck along, Horace."

But why now? Why after all these years?

"It was when I read about Arturo dying," she said. "I'm not frowsting along with this kind of life any longer and nor are the children."

I understood that. When somebody you know dies you take stock.

"He used to talk to me," she said. "He said you'd never be any different."

She'd tried to make it different once or twice before, the way you do at a time of crisis. When we knew Lewis wasn't going to die of polio we had a sort of reunion with mutual promises and the lot. I remember just as I was starting to enjoy the emotion of living a new life and being thoughtful in future I noticed that she'd gone outside and shut the garage doors. This was only a part of her beginning to do things for me but it was the wrong thing. Shut doors is like wearing a hat. I went out afterwards and opened them but without fastening them so that she might think the wind had blown them open.

"Your bank manager didn't know we weren't married," she said.

I know he didn't know for God's sake.

" 'Oh, so he's a bachelor, then!' he said," she said.

This is how I got the news.

I'm not taking this out of the hat as they say in scripting circles, this was the biggest news I'd ever had too. *I am a bachelor!*

"I didn't know he knew I'm not married to Edna," I said. "I thought he thought there was a divorce!"

"The children were there," Tres said then.

"Oh my God!"

"That's what I thought," Tres said. "Do you know what Fiona said? 'Now we don't have to keep it from you.' They knew. They've always known."

I thought about this. Yes, they have. Of course they have.

"You can come and see them whenever you like," Tres said.

She'd worked it out that she would only want a small allowance from me and she could manage the rest herself.

"I may get married again," she said, "but I want to start writing. I've got an idea for a novel."

This alarmed me. I thought I must try to get mine out before she gets hers out. This is the way writers think when their world's crumbling around them—just as long as the typewriter's still there. Then I thought "Again!" Married again! Because living together and raising a family is the same as marriage whereas you would expect it to be better. It's not better, but it's not worse, either.

"Do you know Sheila counts my french letters?" Cedric told me once.

And that was a marriage you would think was intact. Church, everything.

"Oh by the way, there was a telegram from Norman Freville," Tres said as she went out to bed.

I don't know whether she thought *that* was the punch line. "So he's a bachelor?" that was the punch line. It was like telling Atlas with the world on his shoulders they were sorry but he'd picked up the wrong burden—his was the basket of feathers.

"He wanted to know where you were," she said.

"Has he got some news?"

"I don't think so. Paramount has taken the picture and they're going to spend half a million pounds on it in colour if they can get Sophia Loren."

That, as she realised, is no news. That is kite-flying. You learn to know the difference.

"He wanted to know who you'd gone with," Tres said.

"That was a long telegram?"

"I phoned him. He wanted me to phone him."

Nobody I know in the film business would ask Tres to phone them.

"He didn't want to tell you about Paramount?"

"No, that was just butter. He was funny."

"What do you mean?"

"I don't know. Just funny."

"Did he ask you why I'd gone to Rome?"

"Yes. I couldn't tell him, of course."

"You didn't tell him you couldn't tell him!"

She did.

It was late, I was tired, but I went up to the box and rang
his number. There was a strange girl's voice.

"Who the hell's that?" she said.

He should worry about one countess; he had so many
girls who adored him.

"Horace Spurgeon Fenton?" said Albert's voice on the
line. "Hello, mate. I've got a year's lease on The Grange."

When somebody changes the subject before it's been
broached you know they're uneasy about something.

"You'd better tell me what's happened, Albert."

"We've got a package deal with Paramount," Albert said.
"I put up the idea of two-unit production, Norm liked it and
Paramount went for it. He's in Italy now signing up (he
mentioned twenty top-line film stars)."

"Just tell me what's happened," I said patiently.

"The big advantage is that we cut the budget by a third
and come in three weeks earlier than normal shooting time.
What we do is we use two stages instead of one and while
we're shooting on one the other unit is getting the lighting
and set-up ready for the next scene—the director and artistes
just go backwards and forwards from one to the other. Do
you know how many minutes we get in the can per day?
Ten! Ten minutes! I'm working on the cross-plot now—
was there any message?"

"Who have you got there?" I asked. Who could be
important enough on this earth to justify talking such

a load of crap? The terrible thing was he had mastered it.

"Mary," he said. "You remember Mary—at the White Hart?"

"Honest to God," I heard her say, "and there was me thinking you were shooting a line!"

"Where are you, Horace?" Albert asked. "How did the Italian première go?"

I told him where I was.

"Oh, Gawd!" Albert said. He couldn't hide the bitterness. I should have been in Rome getting shot. "Norm wants to get your opinion about the cast."

"I'm sure he does," I said. "Has he got his gun?"

"It's not in the desk," Albert said. "I'll get him to send it on to you."

"If you can't talk just answer yes or no," I said. "Does he think I've gone to Italy with Jane?"

"Oh yes," Albert said, breezily. "I thought so too. Everybody thought so. I thought he knew otherwise I wouldn't have told him."

"You bastard."

"He doesn't blame you, I knew that," Albert said, "it could have been anybody. She's got his end-money. Twenty thousand pounds. We just added two and two. Tres wouldn't say why you'd gone to Rome and Arturo swore he didn't know you! He thought we were the police! He nearly died!"

"He *did* die!" I said, suddenly seeing Arturo turning grey for the last time with the inquisitorial voices on the phone and that five thousand pounds between himself and ruin.

"Have you seen his obituary?" Albert said. "Nothing about you. You want to go to the memorial service. I'll get a photographer laid on."

What happened next was chilling.

"I'm sorry, caller, your time is up, do you wish to pay for further time?" the operator asked.

"I'll transfer the charge," I said. "Will you take it, Albert?"

"Hello," Albert said. "Are you there, Horace? I think we've been cut off," I heard him say.

"Are you transferring the charge?" the operator asked the other end.

Albert had gone. He'd the jargon, the business, all the wickets. Now he'd even got the trick of cutting off a writer who's asking for a transferred charge call, who might want some definite decision in a minute, who might ask for money, who might try to pin you down, who at any rate is broke and better off the line.

Oh this wasn't money with Albert it wasn't his bill. This was the Irish chambermaid; this was not letting me diminish myself and therefore him with the news that I was not at my luxurious penthouse bedside telephone but in a call-box in a High Street.

In a few brief weeks, months perhaps, Albert had learned more about the film business than I would ever learn or care to know. Not the business itself but the façade, the mystique; this, I began to realise, is as much as anybody knows; this would be enough to enable Albert to plough a dizzy ostentatious furrow of a career in the motion-picture business had that been what he wanted and not merely to con an Irish chambermaid.

The convention of starting at the bottom and working your way up doesn't apply in the film business. I had tried for years to get Lang in as a tea boy, using every contact I had but without success. He couldn't get in without a union ticket and he couldn't get a union ticket until he got in. He had learned cameras, done a photographic course at the Regent Street Poly, made and cut some good 8mm pictures, intelligently and with point. It didn't help, nor did all his enthusiasm.

"He's got a good face, mind you," somebody said.

They were looking at his scar.

I thought about this while I read the Norman Freville

[144]

headlines next day. I was sitting in Arturo's outer office. Popsie and Freda were in the luxury office with the door locked.

WAR HERO SHOOTS OLYMPIC GIRL SWIMMER was the unlikely item.

I didn't know that Norman Freville, D.S.O. and Bar, had spent six hours in the English Channel with much of his skin burnt away or that Jane Chappell had got a bronze for her country. Those were not the things you talked about if you wanted to finish up in a notorious shooting scandal in the middle of the Venice Film Festival.

"Horace," Popsie said.

She had cried herself dry and now she came out with a big cardboard box filled with documents. Would I burn them for her? It was all central heating there and she had nowhere to burn them.

"I'll burn them in my garden," I said.

"Well don't put them anywhere, will you? In the dustbin or anywhere. It's only rubbish but I don't want anybody prying."

Now try to concentrate on this bit. Freda came out with some more documents, letters, memos in Arturo's scrawl. "What about these?" she said.

Popsie looked through them. "No, not those," she said. "They're not important."

(They were not important so they weren't for burning?)

I asked them what they were going to do now.

"It's not certain yet," Popsie said.

She spoke as though it was out of her hands.

I heard the telephone go in the big office while I was having my goodbyes with Freda, fondling a little, saying we'd have to see each other again. I heard Popsie's voice because Freda had also stopped making her willing bitch movements to listen.

"Yes, sir. Yes sir. I've done that. It's all got rid of," she said.

"The accountants are coming in tomorrow," Freda said,

[145]

as if this would explain it to me. She started moving again.

There was some secret thing going on which was over my head at the time. I was waiting for Arturo to come strutting past with one of his obscene greetings.

"Was it a heart attack?" I asked Freda.

"I expect so," she said, absently.

And even that seemed part of the secrecy.


Tres was turning out cupboards when I got back.

"If you're going to make a bonfire I've got some stuff to go on it," I told her.

"So have I," she said.

She had to make a thing of every little thing. She had organised a bridging loan from the bank on the strength of the house sale and intended to move into a hotel if she hadn't found a place by the time the new owner took over. There comes a time when a family rift becomes part of out-siders' arrangements and then suddenly what might have been avoided is made official.

I gloomed in my room, making myself feel sick with French cigarettes. I had never taken a great deal of interest in the non-fiction things and now they seemed to be ending through sheer neglect. Edna with an alternative opening out with Frank Fortin, Tres taking off; Arturo dead. You usually see the beginning again when you come to the end-ings. I was on the Yorkshire moors measuring effluent pol-lution of the river from one of the dye works when Tres's name first came up.

"You must meet my secretary," the sales manager said. "She writes books. Never lets anybody read them."

This is the kind of writing I don't understand. He introduced us later in one of the war-time British Res-taurants.

"You write, don't you?" she said, distastefully.

We sat there hating each other and vowing never to meet

again; both not sufficiently writers to know why we hated having our secret places touched.

I ran out of matches and picked up a piece of paper which I found I hadn't read yet. Nothing unusual in that except this piece was nice. It was better than a million-pound note right then.

*Dear Mr Fenton:*

THE BROWSE HIGH AND LOW

*Confirming our arrangements for the signing party at Leamington Spa on the eighteenth:*

*The event we now learn will be covered by Midland Television and the local press, besides the usual trade paper outlets. The net result in terms of publicity for your books should be considerable.*

*I understand from my secretary that you intend to make your own way to* The Browse High And Low. *We shall cover your expenses of course and we would very much appreciate your staying afterwards to dinner with the four other authors.*

*I look forward to the event and to seeing you again. With very best wishes for a bumper day:*

*Yours:*

*George Wimpole.*

It reminded me that I was a quite famous writer and I took it down to show Tres, not that I expected it would do any good. She was nailing the past fifteen years of our life together into tea-chests as though hammering our coffin.

"Did you see this?" I showed the letter.

"I'm not reading the mail any more," she said.

And as I went out she said: "Don't forget you're in court on the eighteenth."

I pretended I didn't hear her just to spoil the dramatic shape of her day. She had to come up and tell me again.

"I've taken care of it," I said, as though I took care of everything.

I had posted a letter from Paris with a Paris postmark excusing my absence from court on the grounds that I would be working in France for the next few weeks. Getting people who were going on holiday or location abroad to post letters to creditors was not a new trick; it had rebounded a few times when I'd met them the day after writing to them apparently from Tobago.

Tres didn't say anything but she looked at me for a moment from the doorway; the kind of look that bridges years; as if asking herself if she was doing the right thing and deciding that she was. I think she felt also that she was getting off a roundabout that would go on turning just the same and in the same monotonous circle.

Albert came in that night excited but frustrated; as though he'd been given a Rolls Royce but no petrol, which was roughly true.

"I've got Norman's flat for three months," he said.

This was his interpretation of the news that Norman Freville had been sent for trial and was not to be given bail.

"What about your job here?" I asked him.

He said he would keep it up until he got some kind of deal going. His mother would see to that. What kind of deal can a milkman get going?

"Have you got any stories that I could set up?" he asked me. "I've got a strong connection with Paramount now. I was talking to their story editor in Hollywood this afternoon. Do you know what? They've never heard of you."

I showed him the letter inviting me to autograph books.

"This kind of thing doesn't hit the headlines, Horace," he said.

He sat there for a moment thinking up something that would. I felt uncomfortable. Albert was changing and it wasn't for the better. I tried to tell him about Tres selling the house and my being a bachelor but he shut me up. Soon he came up with the idea that I should take Freville's flat over until we got something started.

"You can invite all the top people in," he said. "He's got cupboards full of drink."

"What about Mrs P.?" I asked. More than posterity did I want Norman's char to know that I was not a typist.

"I've sacked her," Albert said. "Mary's running it."

I laughed for so long it was like hiccups, I couldn't stop, I needed it. It ended when Tres's bedroom door slammed. That's how you get misunderstood. I brought him down to the level of my personal troubles.

"It's all for the best, Horace," he said. "You'll never do any good while you're pigging it here and the other place. Whatever they give you to write or adapt comes out bills, kids, troubles—they told me! That's not what the film industry wants. There's a big swing away from the kitchen sink. It's glamour again now—have you got anything would suit Kim Novak?"

Only the nailed tea-chests in the hall got through to him and touched him. They were real and not talk. He looked around, suddenly conscious of where we'd been dreaming these past few years.

"She keeps the place nice, doesn't she," he said, "old Tres."

It was a bit late to think about that.

"We'll talk her out of it. I'll send mum round. She can't move away! Where else could I go at this time of the night?"

I decided to let him run me round to his place and then I'd walk back. I wanted to piss on his tow-bar suddenly. While we stood doing it he said: "You don't want to go gadding up to Leamington Spa. Stay with Tres and the kids. You ought to stay with them more, Horace."

He shook his oversize penis as if to emphasise it and the drops fell off like tears.

# 13

# Old Angie

A NUMBER OF THINGS punctuated the days before the eighteenth. We were living in a sort of packed-up and ready to go state, except that I didn't know where I was going. It wasn't like an ordinary family breaking up; I had always been separate. But I loved them all. I even started to get fond of particular cats and found out their names, Daphne and Spurgeon (they all had their names on brass discs attached to their collars). Daphne was the one who brought in the big rats out of the coal yard and left them for the rest to devour or leave spread over the carpet. She was the huntress and the provider. Spurgeon secretly loved her. She was pastel-tabby and he was dog-eared and black. I expect some kind of identification went on there the way it does with humans and animals.

I started shutting the garage doors and putting carpet slippers on. I had a meal with Tres and the children several times. I sat and read a book once in the living room. I watched television occasionally. Seeing something particularly bad one evening I got an idea for turning my Paris trip into a play. I could see my photograph on the cover of the Radio Times.

> Horace Spurgeon Fenton at last turns his giant talent to the dwarf medium . . .

What I had already worked on was the stock series.

Hassan stands at the bar, the ventilator fans stir the sticky heat, a beautiful half-dressed girl pushes through the beads hanging by the door with a gun in her hand. Does the name Fennimore mean anything to you? Hassan nonchalantly taps out his cigarette ash down her bra.

I went down to the library to have a whisper with old Angie. Some lout was pestering her but she got rid of him. Girls seem so wasted when they're with other men.

"That's Stephen," she said. "He's very jealous."

She took me over to Religion—which was always deserted—in case he looked in the window. She was engaged to Stephen. It is a convention of the well-bred English girl that she never has sexual intercouse with the boy she's engaged to. Angie was not a conventional girl at all but she was strict about this one thing.

I had a list of the French things I wanted words and phrases for to cover the Paris episode.

"You're better off without them, Horace," she whispered. "You're much more convincing when you don't use foreign words but just confess your ignorance. That green thing is part of your charm I don't have to tell you. The more authentic you are the phonier you sound."

"Thanks," I whispered.

The chief librarian was coming over.

"Ask me some questions about religion," she said.

It guaranteed a guilty silence.

"Everything all right, Miss Lilley?" the librarian asked. "You've people waiting."

"You're characters could be better—a description or something," she whispered when he'd gone. "I can never see them."

Old Angie has a slightly lop-sided face with a touch of Sherlock Holmes about the eyes and nose and because she thinks she isn't pretty she keeps the whole thing downwards and talks towards the ground but occasionally having to lift her lashes at you to see if you've walked away. This permanent stoop in her neck has resulted in a big blob of brown

[151]

hair settling over one of her eyes—the effect in total is shifty but kind of nice. She has fair-sized breasts—which I've never seen naked because I'm not a breast man—child-bearing hips and a nice round, friendly bum. I am basically a bum man, but only girls' bums. Her tweed skirts are not often tight but move a little just above her knees which are big but well-shaped. She has nice calves and ankles though a little thick. And if I did this with every character you would have a fifty-shilling book on your hands.

"What else?" I said.

"You don't put enough actual sex in your stories," she whispered.

"You mean descriptions of how it feels, sensually, to have intercourse?"

"Yes. People know how *they* feel but they like to know how other people feel." Just talking about it with her my mind crimsoned and bloated and firmed into a mental erection. "It's important," she said. "You ought to think about it. As a novelist I mean. For instance do you know what a girl gets from riding a horse?"

"No wonder you keep looking at the floor," I whispered.

She turned scarlet. "I can't talk like this to anybody else."

Who wants to talk like this?

"I should have married a writer," she said.

She talked as though she was already married.

"*You* haven't been out for ages," she said then.

She'd been working for me all the summer and I hadn't even bought her a beer. I was on the point of telling her about the signing party at Leamington but then didn't. Nearly told her about Tres leaving and Edna having another interest and my being free—but then didn't. You don't buy a dinner for the girl who will do it for a sandwich.

"What are you doing tonight?" I asked her.

"I have to see Stephen tonight."

"Have to?"

"Yes. I'm sorry, Horace—I did cut it down to three times

a week for you. Now I do nothing most of the time and have to pretend all sorts of things to him. I can't go out in case you ring."

"I didn't know that, did I?" I said.

She laughed at me. "I didn't expect you to know it." Then she said: "I've got three weeks holiday coming up."

"We ought to go somewhere," I said.

Her eyes came up and she forgot that she thought she wasn't pretty. She really was.

"Can I hold you to that?" she said.

I promised her that she could.


When I got back to the car Albert in his white coat and milkman's cap was loading tins of fruit into the boot of my car from his float.

"Drive round to Napier's restaurant," he said, "and back into their yard."

"I've got work to do, Albert."

"You'll be away in half an hour. Can I have that box?"

It was the big cardboard box with all the papers from Arturo's office which I'd promised Popsie I would burn for her. Albert was already emptying the contents loose into the boot.

"Don't let it blow about for God's sake," I said. "They're top secret."

He stacked the tins of fruit into the box and closed my boot.

"See you," he said.

He drove off quickly with that elevator whine that electric milk floats make, his coat blowing out the side. He seemed very worried.

I backed into Napier's yard and waited for twenty minutes. With my job, fortunately, waiting is never time wasted. I started working out the crime story set in Paris. I don't like crime stories, I never believe in them, but I'm good at them. I never have anybody with a gun. I had worked out a good way of disposing of a body and triggering a mystery. There would be a car crash which I couldn't yet see; but I could see the detective—my Paris bod—coming in to report. The driver was dead. Pity, another road casualty.

"Not quite, M'sieu. . . . He has been dead three days!"

Da-da-da-daaaah! This is enough to give you a whole TV play.

"All right, mate," Albert said, as he appeared from the back door of the restaurant. He went to my boot and I didn't bother to get out. I saw him go in with the box of tinned fruit and a little later come out counting banknotes. He went and closed the boot of my car but took overlong doing it. I have to sacrifice form for content here. I have to be explicit.

"Albert," I called.

"All right, mate."

He strolled round to my door looking through some papers which I thought were milk accounts or something.

"What's top secret about these, then?" he asked me.

They were Arturo's papers. I took them away from him.

"Don't read them. They're nothing. Only rubbish. I promised her faithfully I wouldn't let anybody see them."

"I'm only a milkman!" Albert said. He said things to suit himself. He certainly didn't really believe that.

"Do us a favour, cocker," he asked me. He took out the banknotes and counted out five. "You know all about wiring money—send Mary five quid for me, will you?"

"Are you keeping her?"

"Only till something breaks," he said. "I took her away from her job, didn't I?" He looked worried again. "Funny girl. Got some funny ideas. I'm not sure I haven't made a mistake there, Horace."

I started the engine but he leaned in and switched it off.

"There's no parking in the High Street. Leave it here and we'll have a coffee when you get back."

It takes all of twenty minutes to wire money. When I got

back he was already in his float which was now parked outside the restaurant yard.

"I'm a bit pressed, Horace," he said, as though I had suggested the whole thing. "I tell you what I've done for you—I've got all that rubbish in with my empties. We've got an incinerator at the dairy. I'll burn it as soon as I get back. Ta ta, mate."

That was how it was done.


I was going to bed early that night. I made a false start on the TV play and was too tired and flat to make another. It wouldn't sell anyway and even if it did they'd take too long to pay. You get these extravagant ideas but the mood doesn't last long and you go back to commissioned work. Get a hundred or two in advance and you've got to write the bloody thing. I couldn't imagine working any other way any more. I lost the art of writing for pleasure. I'd rather be cleaning windows were it not for the money. I never told my pupils this.

"It is the most wonderful life you can imagine," I told them. "You live where you like and no getting up in the mornings. You have an immediate entrée to any strata of society, mixing with titles, royalty, artists. Lovely models clamour to be seen with you."

Tres came in just as I was about to get undressed. She was wearing her coat over her nightdress.

"Another five minutes and I should've been in bed!" I said.

She apologised. Lewis and Fiona had woken her up. They must have been quiet, I didn't hear them.

"They're worried about you," she said. "What are you going to do, Horace?"

"What about?"

"There!" she said. "That's exactly what I told them. We're going! We're leaving here! You don't even think about it, do you? No, you don't. You'll just drift down to

[155]

that lot on housekeeping day and there won't be anywhere for you to drift back to and you'll just stick there. Back where you started, Horace."

"Do you want me to stay with you, then?" I asked her.

"What do you mean, stay with us? You're not with us. You're not with anybody, Horace. What are you looking for? What is it you can't find?"

"I shall know when I've got the money for it," I said.

"You talk like a third-rate thriller. Nobody can talk seriously to you. It's right what Fiona said: You're only truly yourself when you're snoring. . . ." For about ten minutes. She didn't often speak like that any more and she dried up quite quickly as though realising it was time she had already wasted.

"Who's going to be at the autographing?" she asked.

That was new. That was her first new line. She'd always wanted to meet an author; a famous one. We never came across them the way we lived. And if there was a rare occasion, like the publisher's one and only party I was ever invited to, it didn't occur to me to take Tres. It's a bit restricting.

I hazarded a guess at Henry Williamson (she was *Tarka the Otter* mad) and a few others.

"I suppose you'll be taking one of your tarts," she said.

This was the closest she could bring herself to asking me to take her. I didn't pick it up. Had I done so, things would have been different—though not necessarily better.


I was in bed with the light out when Albert threw a stone at the window and broke it.

"You bastard!" I called out to him.

"Sorry, mate!"

I could just see his face upturned in the darkness. I went down and let him in.

"I wondered if I could make a call?" he asked.

It was early but it was one o'clock.

[156]

"To Mary," he said. "She gets frightened sleeping there alone. Well, it's her own fault."

This obscure remark was my first clue to what he had been trying to get her to do now that there was a luxury flat and plenty of drink; why he felt he might have made a mistake with her; what her funny ideas were. He had set her up in Freville's Flat.

"Do you mind if I take it alone, mate?"

I went to the bathroom for ten minutes. When I returned he was sitting at my desk, his eyes narrowed, contemplating infinity.

"Did you get through?" I asked him.

"What?" he said. "Oh, yes, thanks. Ta. What does an Assistant Producer do?"

I didn't know. I'd never heard of it.

"There's Assistant Producers," he said. "There must be."

"Associate Producer," I told him, remembering.

"That's better," he said. "Associate Producer. That's what I meant. What does he do?"

I told him as much as I knew. Associate Producers weren't born until a picture had started. Then they did all the donkey work for the producer; running around, seeing people, administration, money, personnel.

"Does he know everything the producer knows?" Albert said. "Is he in the producer's confidence?"

"If it was you," I said.

"He could, then? I mean you couldn't say he didn't?"

"Who couldn't?"

"What are you doing on Sunday?" he said.

"Only writing."

"Well as you're doing nothing how about running me down to the coast? I'll buy the petrol."

I said no for five minutes and finally yes.

"I've got something big on," he told me. "Tell you what it is if it comes off."

"What about this window?" I asked him.

He looked at the hole in the glass. It was a fairly neat one, about three inches and not very jagged.

"Waste not want not," he said.

He picked up the telephone and dialled the police station.

"There's been a shooting," Albert told them. "I'll get in touch with the newspapers in the morning," he told me at the front door. "If we do it now it'll look suspicious. They'll be able to check with the police tomorrow—okay?" He did that thing of walking away and coming back with a mock-pray: "And Horace—don't fluff it!"

It could have been Al Dalgleish.

I waited fifteen minutes in a nervous tizz. Then not until I heard the police car outside did I remember that I'd have to wake up the family. Tres and the kids have never understood how the police and the dog handler arrived almost coincidentally with the sound of the shot (I clapped my hands). Tres said she always felt safer at night after that.

"Tell me exactly what happened, sir," the sergeant said.

I reconstructed it for him, more or less. We had the "have you got any enemies" thing and whether I had heard any drunken singing; could it have been schoolboys, had it happened before, was there a family row of any kind. I was suitably baffled for a motive but Tres and the children kept a tactful silence as if they didn't want to involve anybody's husband or boy friend.

"Who was with you?" the sergeant got to at last.

I told him.

"Who?" he exclaimed.

"Albert Harris," I said.

He looked at a constable who laughed.

"Get Jimmy back," the sergeant said, tiredly.

Jimmy was the dog handler who had picked up a scent in the railway coal yard and was following it down the line.

"Bill!" the sergeant called up the stairs.

There came a yell of pain and the constable whom Tres had asked to check the rooms came down gripping one of his hands where the Monster had bitten it to the bone practically. We could still hear her yelling with laughter.

Tres and I both apologised and tried to explain. You could never explain it, though. Autistic children always convince strangers that somebody should have kept them under control.

In the morning the car came from the psychiatric home and took Diana away—our Diana. Tres and Lewis and Fiona were all in the living-room crying together. I couldn't get near them or enter into it. It was nothing to do with biting the policeman, it was what Tres had arranged and not before time.

"I just want to forget her now," Tres said, when I made her some coffee.

"I've just *made* some coffee," Lewis said.

Fiona came in with a tray of coffee, looked at us, went back. That was our last combined operation as a family.

Whatever publicity Albert might have achieved the next day fell quite flat for there had been a mail train robbery involving millions of pounds and the newspapers were filled with it, each edition trying to cap the last with the amount involved. There was a jubilant, public-holiday feeling everywhere as the hold-up took the place of the weather between total strangers. Even Tres was smiling as the telecasts came over. For us particularly, living between the cracks of a weekly and monthly and quarterly ordered society, there was a feeling of achievement; that the Spanish Main was still there and some of the gold had come to us night people at last instead of to them. It was a blow against the seven-day makers. It was a battle in a war that we could understand. It was crime without a knighthood in mind.

It was the 6th of August, 1963.

# 14

# A Leap of Frogs

I DROVE ALBERT DOWN to Angmering-by-Sea on the Sunday for an appointment with Arturo Conti's titled executive friend. I didn't know where we were going until we were almost there and he told me. We had spent the whole of Saturday evening cleaning my Hurricane. For the past two weekends I had sent Edna's money by post and excused myself the pictures chore; it was a welcome tailing-off operation. I had got news by letter from my eldest daughter Lang that Mr Fortin had bought Edna a new coat and that she was using his washing machine.

"Do you think it's wise, dad?" Lang had written.

Now parked along a quiet sea road at Goring Albert got in the back of my car and I put on his milkman's cap with the insulating tape stuck round it.

"And you'd better wear your sunglasses," Albert said, "in case he recognises you."

I put them on. Whatever Albert had in mind—and he wouldn't tell me—I didn't want to be recognised as part of it.

I sat parked in the drive of the titled executive's seaside mansion for two hours. When Albert finally came out with the tycoon they were laughing together.

"Would your man like a drink before you go?" the titled one asked.

"No, no," Albert said. "I don't believe in spoiling them."

I drove him back to the sea road at Goring but I noticed that he was reluctant to come in the front of the car again; irritated when I took off the milkman's cap.

"What did you see him about?" I kept asking.

"I want to think, Horace," Albert said. "Call in at my London place, will you?"

He sat there brooding and saying not a word for the length of the Sunday jam on the A24. When I stopped outside Norman Freville's flat he sat there for a moment as though searching for a vital clue.

"Who is Al Dalgleish?" he asked me at last.

I said: "A friend of mine."

My tone must have indicated my dwindling patience. He asked me to go up and have a noggin and he called me "old boy".

The flat was not quite the torture chamber I remembered. There were pictures of every famous face in the business all signed with love to Albert in the same handwriting —his. The drinks had been brought out of the kitchen and displayed on the sideboard. Central on the desk as Albert took his place behind it was a large photograph of Albert, Arturo Conti and Marilyn Monroe with their arms around each other; so cleverly cut out and faked that you would never know it unless you knew Albert. Quite half the pictures had been lifted from my room the night he pretended he wanted to use the telephone. He admitted it cheerfully when I mentioned it.

"What use were they stuck in a drawer?" he said.

Mary was not there but astonishingly Albert's mother came in from a walk and started cooking her dinner.

"I spend half me time in the bathroom," she told me over her dry martini. "It's the one reason I don't regret leaving the caravan. We couldn't bath for a year at a time."

And when Albert was out of the room she smiled at me and said: "He's done well, hasn't he? Keep by him and he'll help you, Horace. He never forgets a friend."

When Albert thought I'd had enough to drink he

pumped me about Al Dalgleish, what Arturo Conti was engaged on at the time of his death and why I was going to Rome. I told him. He was right, I had had enough to drink.

"Did you ever speak to Ricki Angelo?" Albert asked.

"Who?"

"The man you were going to collect that five thousand from? The chap in Rome?"

"No," I said. "Was that his name?"

"You must have known his name, Horace."

I don't remember names. "It was on the envelope if I wanted it."

"What envelope?" Albert said.

"The letter of authority. For me to collect the money."

Albert had turned red with oncoming excitement. "Where is it?" he said.

"I don't know—"

"You must know! Think! Did you give it back to his office?"

"No—what use is it? He's dead."

Albert said: "The deal isn't dead, Horace! You've got to find that letter—look in your pockets."

"You couldn't do anything with it—nobody could except Arturo."

Albert contained himself. "A deal is a deal. It doesn't matter whether Arturo puts it through or Charlie Staircase. Do you think Rock Willis gives a damn who he gets that five thousand pounds from?"

"Who's Rock Willis?"

Albert sprawled in the swivel chair, his foot up on the desk, and looked at me pityingly as if he now knew why I would always be poor.

"You've been working all these years in the diamond fields, Horace, and you've been picking up the gravel."

He clicked his fingers at me. "Give me that letter."

I told him that if I'd had it I wouldn't have given it to him. It would be like betraying Arturo's trust.

"I'm Arturo's Associate Producer, Horace, therefore I

have the authority to carry through the deal on the picture."

"What picture?" I asked him.

That stumped him; he didn't know. I refused to tell him. I didn't know either.

"I'm doing this for you as well as me," he said.

"I don't want you going to prison for me."

"I've been accepted," he said. He told me that the titled executive and his company had accepted him. That they were prepared to give him the same deal they would have given Arturo if he got the American participation signed and settled.

"Why would they do that?" I said.

"There are about twenty-five good reasons why they daren't refuse," Albert said. "And you had them all in the boot of your car."

I still wouldn't give him the letter. Mrs Harris was resting on Norman Freville's bed. We looked in on her to say good-bye.

"Did you find out which hospital the Countess was in?" Albert asked her.

"It's a hospital in Venice," she said, "I've got it written down."

"I'll send you some money to wire her flowers," Albert said. "Don't forget to put my name."

"Don't take a day off work, Albert," she said. "You can't risk losing that job till you've got something firm." And to me, she said: "Turn the greens down for me, love."

Albert didn't mention the letter again on the drive back in a way that left it important. Also without mentioning it I tried to talk him out of it. Even if he got into the film business he would find it a lot of hard work and frustration.

"You're wrong," he said, "it's just talking. And I like talk-ing. Knowing how to use people. Getting them in your power."

"What's that got to do with making pictures? It's a highly technical job—artistic, too."

"I use technicians and artists," he said. "People like you."

[163]

"The producer's job is intricate and complicated. It takes years to master. Budgets, breakdowns, cross-plots, timing, studio rental, set-building, location administration, casting and costing."

"You don't know Popsie's private address, do you?" Albert said as though I'd reminded him of some little thing.

I got him back to the caravan site by about eleven that Sunday night and we passed water on the tow-bar by habit. His lights were on and I could hear music.

"Who's here?" I asked him.

He looked at me for a moment in a chess-moving way. "Horace, what are you going to do when Tres moves?"

I told him I didn't know yet.

"How would you like this caravan and my *au pair* girl?" Albert said.

"What *au pair* girl?"

He indicated silence and led me to one of the caravan windows. We peered inside. There was a blue television light coming from the main room of the van. The kitchen was lighted only by the reflection of this. A girl sat naked in the sink washing herself and singing. It was Mary, the Irish chambermaid. We watched her screw up the corner of the flannel and twist it into her ears.

When we'd moved away Albert said: "I won't bother about the other thing now. You can have her and the van —costs you five pounds a week—if you give me that letter to Ricki Angelo."

I accepted.

"Where's the letter?" he asked.

I told him I expected it was in my holdall; I'd emptied my pockets since I got back from Paris.

"I'll go round to your place and get the letter," he said. "You go in now and break the ice—I'll give you an hour. You have to get her drunk the first time—oh Christ, there's no drink. Well let's do it tomorrow. And one word of warning—don't let her know you're not married." He said it bitterly. "I've found out a few things about the Irish. You

know why she wanted her sisters over? As bridesmaids!
That's the way they work. They send the prettiest over to
start the ball rolling and then before you know it the whole
lot are over here. You're infested with sister-in-laws and
stupid relations. You know Bert at the dairy? That's what
happened to him. The country's riddled with Irish sisters-
in-law all set up as solid as supermarkets and breeding like
flies."

"Let's get the letter, anyway," I said.

As we walked to the car a man came out of the trees.

"Lovely weather!" he called.

"Piss off," Albert said, pleasantly. "Spanish f—— luna-
tic," he explained.


On the eighteenth-minus-one I telephoned Diana the
high priestess. She screamed.

"And hello to you," I said.

"I *knew* it was you! I knew it was *you*! I've just finished
it! Just this minute! Remember that big piece of rock? I
knew I would hear from you or meet you or something. I
never thought about the telephone because you never ring.
This is fantastic, Horace, do you realise that? Five months
I've been chipping away and—I can't believe it! Basil's
dead!"

"Who?"

"Do you know who it turned out to be?"

"Basil?"

"No, my Rutland Man—" She said a name, I ought to
damn well know it but it's gone—she was always on about
him. "The Aztec fertility god! I didn't know it. He was
already there, in the stone! He came out in the last three
weeks, chip by chip—he hated it. He stands there in the
back garden glowering. The neighbours are frightened, I'm
not joking. They say it's the best thing I've ever done. Do
you know I've got the feeling I didn't do it at all. Like you
feel about your writing sometimes. As if you're just uncover-

ing something that was there—ugh! Do you get goose-pimples? Yes, you do, I remember! When am I going to see you—touch you? O Horace! This is marvellous. I'm crying."

Basil was her brother, the one with the long hair. He died suddenly from anthrax, a disease that kills animals. Basil caught it from a bristle tooth brush. I learned this in passing as we drove to Leamington Spa.

I suppose the 18th of August 1963 was a fate day; you don't recognise it as such until it's too late. Tres and the children chose it for looking at a new flat in Wimbledon. She chose that particular day because I hadn't suggested that she came with me to the book-shop opening. I could have scrubbed it and gone with them to look at the flat; half wanted to. The other thing that was happening was that my name was being called out in court and the registrar was reading my letter from Paris and some sneaky clerk from his office was getting up to say how could I be in Paris when somebody had put a shot through my window the other night when I was working. It had got publicity in the week-end local paper.

*"A Mr Horace Sperjon was writing a thriller in his bedroom the other night when somebody fired a shot through the window!"*

One or two other things had happened before the eighteenth which I had not recognised as a burning fuse. I clinched the caravan deal not with Albert but with Mary. Albert had gone to Italy. I got this from the milkman a few days after I had given Albert the letter to Ricki Angelo.

"He's gone on holiday," the milkman said.

"He's had his holiday," I said. Albert's holidays had always been an increase in company promotion, visiting cards, wallpaper inventors.

"He bought mine," the milkman said. "I'd rather work to tell you the truth."

This had to be Albert's colleague with an Irish invasion on his hands.

I found an off-licence in a neighbouring town which had not had one of my cheques and got a crate of vintage cider, beer, whisky, gin and fizzes for dilution. I took the lot up to the caravan during the evening.

Mary opened the door and couldn't find her voice for a moment; had to swallow. It wasn't surprise, it was that she hadn't spoken to anybody for days.

"Thank God for somebody!" she said. "Is he not back yet?"

She took me inside. On a table by the television set was a tent of white brocade and lace. She was making her wedding dress. What I had in mind was not going to be easy.

She talked about Albert incessantly through half the cider and most of the whisky. His great future, where they intended to live, how many children she wanted, housework, cooking, dress-making came next; she talked to me as to a neighbour over the fence; as to a woman. As the alcohol got into her blood she came to the confidences and the fears.

"The only thing about him is he's too broad-minded, too trusting. Do you know what he wanted to do? Only let one of his friends stay the night at the flat when I was there alone! It's a compliment to me, I suppose, that he trusts me that much, but it's not right. I had to fight him on it! Do you know if he saw us here together now he wouldn't give a damn. Do you like this, Mr Fenton?"

She held the dress against herself and trod in stately fashion the length of the caravan—thirty feet through living room, kitchen and bedroom and back again. After another bottle she was swirling it round and I managed a brief dance with her. It was my first physical contact. She swayed a bit when I let go of her.

"You're going to have to go," she said. "I feel dizzy. I'll have to lay down."

"Albert has asked me to take this place over," I told her. "Would you mind if I look at the bedroom?"

[167]

"Not at all," she said. "It's through there."

I went and looked at it on my own, came back.

"Thanks," I said. "I'd better be going, then."

"You're very gentlemanly," she said.

I kissed her. It was sheer temper.

"Don't do that!" she said. "I've got no will power at all when I've been drinking."

"Nor have I," I said.

I took her into the bedroom and on to the bed.

"Don't touch me, will you? Promise you won't touch me?"

Of all the human activities this is the one that seems most vital at the time and is most easily forgotten. This one I remember for its perfection. The weightlessness of it. The levitation of the body by the sliding paradise of the mind.

"You won't touch me?" she kept saying.

I kept promising that I wouldn't.

A nightingale started up outside.

I didn't know then that caravans rock.


EXT: BOOKSHOP WINDOW: DAY

Open with panning shot of five large portraits of famous authors, the last of which is Charles Fenton on which camera holds. I won't milk it. The letter had come to me by mistake.

"I'm terribly sorry, Mr Fenton," George Wimpole said.

He looked about fifteen and he was the literary editor. I swear there's a teenage conspiracy to take over. It only remains to go into court and find a teenage judge (okay, dad, speak up!).

"I may as well sign some of your books," I told Charles Fenton, "I'm always being credited with them."

"And me yours," he said, less happily I thought.

It was the Royal Première fiasco over again but Diana took it well. They had no books of mine for me to sign and she offered to scour the town and find some. I gave her a pound and she went. There were not yet any customers and the writers stood in a circle which had opened at my brief introduction but had now closed again as they discussed George Orwell, a dead writer.

"He was not genuinely working-class," a woman novelist was saying.

"I write science fiction but I'm not genuinely a Martian," a man said.

"But you don't adopt attitudes, Frank."

"But I do, Dorothy! I hate earthmen. Earthmen speak with forked tongue!"

It was nice hearing writers talking. I started to feel glad I came anyway. I never meet writers. I don't think they did very much. They seemed happy and talkative and laughed a lot as though they knew that everything they said or even didn't say would be completely understood. Diana came back with half-a-dozen of my Caxton Drakes.

"I'm not going to sign those!"

"But you must, Horace!" the woman novelist said. "Don't be a snob about markets—it's all money, it all takes a hell of a lot of doing."

"You're right, Dorothy," I said.

"This is smashing stuff," Charles Fenton said, flipping the pages. "I wish I could do it. I need some catch-crops."

"Don't we all, dear."

"What are they paying for half-hour series now?"

"Three hundred."

"I got two-fifty—I think it depends on things."

"Do you find you get good plotting exercise out of doing these thrillers?" Charles Fenton asked me.

"It's been invaluable," I told him. "I only need an initial situation now and I can spin fifty thousand words quicker than a lot of people can copy-type."

"That's what I badly need," he said. "I'm poor on invention."

"Try the morning papers," Dorothy said. "I tell you a trick I used to use. . . ."

It was great.

"And what do you do besides look gloriously beautiful?" I heard somebody ask.

An older writer was smiling at Diana with bright, eggshell blue eyes. I'd like to tell you his name but I suppose, as my pupil says, it is not the done thing. I can never use initials, either; when I read that initials come in and sit down and have a cup of tea I think of Alice in Wonderland. Diana told him.

"Oh no!" he exclaimed. "That's marvellous! Did you hear that, Dorothy?"

"Are you a real sculptor?"

"Do you earn money at it?"

It's not a materialist outlook. We haven't much time for people who play at the arts.

"Not much," Diana said.

"A living?"

"Oh yes."

"Well, that's everything!"

"Now come and sit down here, Diana," the elder said. "Clear off you lot. This meeting is most fortuitous."

"For him, he means—watch out, dear!"

"No, leave them alone. He's writing a book about a sculptor."

"Just a little bit, that's all," the elder told Diana. "He's not a main character and his job doesn't come into it very much but it must be right. Don't know a damn thing about them. What sort of things do they do? You know, everyday things. What time do they get up in the mornings? Who's likely to come knocking on their door? What do they worry about—give me a typical day. I'd be most grateful."

The scene was familiar; Diana and the old man, she leaning forward to him, brightly animated.

"Well it's very hard work," Diana was telling him. "Sheer physical hard work—I mean prisoners do it."

"Of course they do! Stone-breaking! You don't think of that when you see some smooth and polished body in blue granite or marble or something. What about different stone? Is there much to it? Give me an anecdote. They're the most useful, I find."

"No end of accidents," Diana said.

I got goose pimples. This is not hindsight. I got goose pimples when she said that.


"Enjoying it?"

George Wimpole was smiling at me. I don't know how long he had been watching me. He was not fifteen at all I discovered as the afternoon went on but completely capable, putting customers at their ease, liasing between the writers and the shop people, giving us all sherry. "I'll get you out on the next bee," he said. They had done one paperback of mine, now out of print—it had sold nothing.

"You'll write a best-seller," Charles Fenton told me. He had sensed that I had felt at a disadvantage and had been reading one of my Drakes almost solidly since Diana came in with them. "You've got the touch," he said. "Not that it's a good thing in itself, the best-seller—none of us wants to be pop—but it does bring all your old books on the counter. All the things you wrote when there was nobody listening."

He had written six novels, I now learned, four of them still unpublished, before bringing out the football story. When we talk and think about a flash in the pan we're inclined to ignore what else is in the pan besides the flash; how long it took to ignite.

I hadn't talked much myself since trotting out the "missed university by three streets" line and George Wimpole saying as everybody laughed: "I always liked that."

I was arrested by the police while they were still arranging the lights for the television recording. In the movie if I ever sell rights there will be a fight in front of the camera and a chase up to the attic but it was much more civilised in fact. Albert's two inches of publicity about the shooting

[171]

breaking the news that I was not in Paris had rebounded on an irritated County Court Judge.

"I'm tired of people who consistently treat the courts with contempt and get away with it," he was reported as saying. This of course got two full columns and national coverage. "I am issuing a warrant for Mr Fenton's arrest," he said. "I want it executed today if he has not gone back to Paris."

The solitary policeman, who wandered diffidently into the shop representing all that mass of power, I mistook at first for a customer. I heard him asking for Mr Fenton, I saw him talking to Charles and then quite suddenly recognised the situation as he came across.

"Could I have a moment, sir?" he said.

"What is it, parking?" Dorothy said. And then when she knew she burst into rich laughter; she could have been a hospital matron or a member of parliament. She was famous for intelligent murder stories. "Horace that's marvellous!" she cried. "What splendid timing! I wish to God things like this happened to me. Who've you got on your side?"

There were about twenty people laughing about it. Instead of feeling embarrassed I felt that my stature had increased, as though I had arranged the whole thing to enliven the afternoon.

"He always does things like this," Diana told the elderly writer proudly.

It amused them again that neither I nor the policeman knew what the court case was about.

"And yet he accepts it so beautifully!"

"Pointed-headed bastards on their little noddy bikes!" I heard Charles Fenton mutter angrily, as I was escorted out. That's the first thing he's said, I thought, that reflects his writing. *You suck up to them when you're sober, you hit them when you're drunk.* There's something in it. Charles was on his sixth sherry.

I drove my car to the police station. The bobby escorted me on his bike as though I were Royalty in Leamington for the waters. It was straightforward and they were all nice about it but it still took half-an-hour. I had to keep showing them how to fill in the form and even then they got the issuing officer's name in place of mine.

"Sorry about all this Mr Richardson," the young policeman said at one stage.

We had a poor dinner but a happy one in an olde worlde hotel. They had stewed the steak without braising it or seasoning it and what you got was what falconers call "washed meat". They use it for keeping their peregrines constantly hungry by boiling out the goodness. A lot of people prefer this.

"Give them good food and you go bankrupt!" Arturo's millionaire catering friend once said in retaliation. "What they want is rubbish on cracked plates." It had taken him years to master the secret of what people wanted.

I got the older writer's autograph. Nobody had any paper or a pen and he borrowed the waiter's pencil and drew a mock cheque on the back cover of my cheque book.

"I'm not a gonner, you know!" he said as we all watched him write. He had sensed my reverence and awe but preferred Diana's sweet body-odours.

He wrote (I lost it immediately):

THE BANK OF GOD PROMISES TO PAY
Horace Spurgeon Fenton

£Everything he deserves.
(Forgive him all his sins except monopolising his lovely sculptress)

Signed:

And he signed it. I expect he had done the same kind of thing before. It was flippant and yet there was in his face as he did it something I'd noticed about the other writers when they were giving their autographs. Something not apparent when film people or show people perform the

[173]

same favour for their fans. The writers all did it carefully as though they were chiselling stone.

The other thing I remember amongst all the talk and laughter was the Yorkshire novelist Frank, who had been pleasant and happy but had said hardly a word suddenly telling us that he had married his first wife because she was pregnant by another man. The woman who was with him—I forget whether or not it was his wife—was shocked. Perhaps she had been inhibiting him.

"You shouldn't tell strangers things like that!"

"They're not strangers, love, they're writers," he told her.

"We don't know how to talk about the weather, do we?" the elder said.

It was probably the happiest day I've spent and to think I nearly lit my cigarette on it. Only one thing spoilt it for me—I wished that Tres was there. I should have brought her into contact with these people years ago. Instead of shutting her off, cutting myself off, trying to live without our own kind. Instead of giving her the wrong end of the stick, the grubby end.

"I found a box of old sanitary towels under your amour's bed," she had told me when she was clearing out Alice's room. "I wondered what was stinking."

I knew about it. Alice wasn't a slut. She was afraid to burn them on Tres's fire, afraid to block up Tres's lavatory, afraid to bury them in Tres's garden.

"You always pretend people are frightened of me!" Tres would say.

They were. I was. She was a bit of rock that took a great deal of chiselling and yet the heart of it, the nature, was always there.

"You poor bugger," she said to me once when I had flu (real flu, not a cold; grey and dying and not even smoking) and she brought chicken broth to me. I had given her the desperate remedy from that Saroyan story about the Armenian waiter who would have died had he not got the strength of the country in him by running without shoes as a boy. It worked and I lived but I shall always remember her compassion and her swearing. She treated me as gently as if I was one of her sick cats that time. She would never normally swear. Either she did it in friendship to identify with me or else she had to be deeply hurt, angry, outraged, driven beyond control to swear. Then she would come out with a word like "fuck" in front of the children and animals. It was her way of saying that I had corrupted her and we could no longer rely on her. It was her way of frightening us.

"What a terrible woman," quite intelligent people would say to me after visiting us casually.

Quietly I crossed them off my list.

"You never stick up for me," she used to say. "I've never heard you say one word in my favour."

About some people one word is worse than useless. I would have had to be a genius to justify her rudeness, a poet to explain her soul. She would switch off a television programme no matter who was watching it with a terrible silent intolerance that was louder than a comment. Nobody would try to switch it on again. Certainly I wouldn't. I would remember the men I knew who developed television and radio for the benefit of humanity. The man who cried the day Hitler went into Austria, the chap who made the first microphone for the first broadcast out of a cocoa tin for Dame Clara Butt to sing into; the man who sweated all night to get Baird's apparatus out of Crystal Palace the night it burned down.

"People think I don't like London but that's not true," says the singing yob to the craven compere as millions breathe their relief. "I do like London—"

Tres would just switch it off.

And I remember the little bit of filth she brought in and washed in weak boracic lotion until it turned out to be an injured frog. A few days later she watched it jump away in the long grass much the way she watched me walk out of her life.

# 15

# God

DIANA WANTED ROCK.

"Where are we?" she said.

I told her.

"Instead of going back," she said, "why don't we drive up to Rutland?"

Everybody had gone. We sat in the coffee lounge of the old hotel. It was nine o'clock in the evening and they were waiting to lock up. Never mind the dinner we had had a lot of drink, good conversation and the spirit was one of adventure and romance—in fact I think she was misreading it. It was not a Rutland Rock spirit as it had been in the club that night. It was that new horizons feeling you get with an old girlfriend when you find yourselves together in a strange place with nobody knowing you any more and a bedroom upstairs. She had on a simple green satin dress about eighteen-eighty, nothing underneath I would say, her red hair straight down to her shoulders.

"No, Horace," she said, reading my eyes.

I told her about being free now.

"That's awful," she said. "You poor thing."

This kind of remark illuminates a relationship.

"We'll stay here tonight and drive up to Rutland tomorrow," I ordered.

She mocked me as she always did when I tried to dominate her. "And then you'll drive home and I might possibly see you in six months' time and in the meantime I've sacrificed my honour for a piece of rock."

Extend this tiny light-hearted bit of possessiveness in a girl and you've got your failed marriage. This was an old theme of hers if you remember. Why didn't we make love? Because I would go away just the same and she couldn't bear that. Not if it was a flesh relationship.

"I'm not going home any more. There isn't a home. Tres has sold up and gone to live in Wimbledon. I'm staying with Albert until I get a flat. My stuff is in the back of the car." Well it was. You can't go into an hotel without a bit of luggage and I had planned this but without relying on it.

"You make it very hard for me, Horace."

This is yes, we all know it.

"I may not do anything," I said, to clinch it and give her something to hope for. "Remember last time at Cedric's?"

"Promise you won't expect anything then?"

I promised. She touched my hand.

"You won't run away again?" she said.

I went across to the desk.

"No rooms, sir, I'm afraid, we're full up." The woman at the desk gabbled it before I got there. They'd been watching us. Making bets probably.

"I just wanted another coffee," I said, "that's all."

This kind of thing makes me shake. It upsets me more than world issues. These old inns make such a thing of reproducing the seventeenth century but the only thing they ever expose is their beams. Where is the spirit that set Fielding burning the midnight candle on *Tom Jones*? They've got the period inns but they run them like period monasteries. The English catering trade wants to spend less time on the old brass and more time on reproduction serving wenches. The kitchens are a lost cause except to the cockroaches, the landlords are waiting to go to bed (disgustingly enough with their *wives*), the chambermaids are already spoken for by the bog priest and the Pope haunts the corridors. The rumbustious visiting squire today would die of malnutrition.

They should repeal the Irish slave trade laws and put down their money for the old Angies of this country; get them fresh out of grammar school. There is more brain, fibre and rich red peasant blood going down the kitchen sink in this country than we can afford to lose.

"No coffee after nine o'clock, sir," guess-who said.

"Colloquial phrases like 'get stuffed' have an increasingly necessary place in our language today," I once told a Literary Society.

We did the grand tour. Only compulsive womanisers need shed tears. Man's search for a place to get horizontal with nobody looking. Keeping up the pretence that you are looking for somewhere to have a picnic (funny, I can't drink lemonade unless I'm completely shut in). As though this is not sufficient strain it is implicit in this situation that you have to meet a series of cynical knowing strangers and keep up a flow of innocent chatter.

"The car has got a squeak, I don't think it will get us back. If we could just put up until the morning. Have you got a telephone so that I can ring the children?"

You begin to think you are the only human being who doesn't lay eggs in the normal way.

"My wife is starting the slipper-bath treatment for her arthritis and we just forgot to book up."

It is worse if you are three times the girl's age.

"Terribly sorry it's so late (it's ten o'clock and you've heard the chains coming off for the last five minutes) but if you could possibly find a room—any room. I'd pay double price."

I wondered if Tres and the children were back yet. If she had decided to take the flat. Whether if I started now I could get there before they'd gone to bed and talk to them.

"I've got one," Diana said, coming back to the car.

We'd got to the stage when the pretences are down and

you've split up to make a desperate two-pronged assault on the bed-and-breakfast houses.

"I said you were my father," Diana whispered as we walked up the privetted garden path. "Unfortunately your room is in the next house—don't ask me why." (You have to pay for two rooms as retribution, is why.)

The first thing was she didn't undress. It didn't seem sinister at first. I was prepared for the fact that it was not going to be easy. The girls I'd been most successful with, like Freda at Arturo's, I had never established any kind of social relationship first; like talking, laughing, philoso-phising, understanding each other, liking each other. Build it this way and these are bricks you have to take down again before you get to essentials. What I did with Diana was, kissed her immediately we got inside the bedroom instead of talking to her, got hold of all her long red hair and pulled her back on to the bed. I was starting a new rela-tionship; she wondered who it was for a minute.

"Let me put this down, then," she said.

She was holding a hot cup of coffee over the back of my head without spilling it. I started again. The bed was thick and soft and springy. I kissed her lightly all over her face and eyes, ran my tongue into her ear, then kissed her properly with my tongue, with everything, with my legs over hers, my hand up and down her green satin dress. I felt that everything was going to be all right.

"Don't worry," she said.

This is one way of doing it. Another way is to tip a bucket of icy cold water over your head. The whole trick is getting your mind off it. Even the word "worry" is anti-procreation.

I went to the bathroom which was across the landing past a room where a child called "Night night" and I called "Night night" back, down three or four stairs—what's that French word when a room is between floors; like maison-ette. Anyway, I stripped right off and stood on tiptoe and bathed myself with hot water for about five minutes, using

[179]

somebody's flannel. As I came out with my clothes the landlady came up the stairs with a cup of coffee.

"Can you take it?" she said. And when I did she whispered conspiratorially: "Dreadful weather!"

Diana was still dressed. She lay on the bed, up on one elbow as if waiting for me.

"Aren't you going to get undressed, sweetheart?"

"Mmm!" she said. She didn't blink at my nakedness (I was holding my stomach in). She took my hand and put it on the mother-of-pearl buttons of her green satin dress.

People have got their own favourite way of doing things. Finding out is fun but it has to be done very delicately and completely by ear.

"This is what I've been missing," she said as I took her dress off. And then, a shade too late: "Being waited on."

You know what came into my head and I'm sure it has yours: her brother was recently dead.

"I'll put the light off," I said.

"You needn't."

So this was a "lights on" girl. I started the kissing and stroking routine but with that much more contact.

"Be peaceful, petal," she said.

Be peaceful? I like it. It's biblical but I like it. She is not easy to draw into fine focus. The words "petal", "blossom" and "flower" were not endearments they were directions for use. Fey, and religious with it. But not Salvation Army religious. Her god was some big granite foreigner. She lay like a sacrifice on the blue Marks and Spencer bedspread with her long red hair over her breast. I felt I ought to chant something. Then what she did—no matter what I did—she gradually slipped over the side of the bed, like blankets do, her head and one hand hanging down to the floor. I'm sure the other hand would have been hanging down too except that I was new; it was gently pressing my head up and down so that my hair brushed her as she moved to meet it.

Crucifixion is unselfish too. We do it for all humanity

who have to stay home watching television every night. She got what she wanted quite suddenly, as when you try to light a damp sparkler with a match on a blowy night.

I got a stiff neck.

"Would your hair grow?" Diana asked me as we drove north through Corby on 6003.

Save me from Aztecs and Eskimos and join me in a vote for long-haired brothers.


Diana screamed as she did whenever God had directed us together again. I ran across the floor of the quarry to her. She was staring half-afraid at a rock.

"I walked straight to it!" she said.

She clasped her hands into a church steeple and pressed it against her mouth, shivered as with goose-pimples.

"It's Basil's memorial," she said. "I knew it was here!"

It was a male organ. Fifteen feet long and a yard thick, it lay embedded horizontally in the soil and sand and shale of the quarry wall. In case there was any doubt she started scraping away the soil from one end with her bare hands in urgent rescue as though it had been suffocating for the past fifty million years and every second counted. A piece of rock which had appeared to be separate from the main piece now was revealed to be joined on. Like a big acorn.

"Perfect!" she exclaimed.

None of your phallic symbols, satirical allusions or blurb-writers' overtones; this had everything except a foreskin.

It chilled me to see the power and the passion in her face. I made some petty admiring comment but she didn't reply. I wasn't there now. I was only the driver again.

"I'll need special transport," she told it.

Now I wasn't even the driver.

I got mad. I could just see her standing in front of it in her garden with her little chisel for the next six months giving it an erection while I picked my nose.

"I'll help you get it out," I said.

[181]

Getting it out didn't mean getting it out any more than making love meant making love. They've all come too far from the caves, these people. She had used her hair on me last night when it was my turn. First like a whip and then holding it near the end like a brush. I laughed. You're not supposed to laugh.

Diana would only give herself to old whatsit, the Aztec fertility god or one of his mates. I think she had had one flesh relationship and the chap had gone off. She wasn't a virgin but she was from then on. In future she would put them where she could see them; in the garden and too heavy to move. Nice girl, mind you. It was just time she was raped for her own good and everybody else's.

We got the stone out together. I tackled the high end and she tackled the low end. What you do merely is scrape away all the loose stuff surrounding it until you get the full contours with some idea of the buried dimension and where it will conveniently break.

"Be careful, Horace, it's ripe," she called up.

She meant that it was loose and ready to fall.

"I'm going to get Mr James and the tackle," she said.

Why should old men put themselves out for a young girl like that? Because to be delicate, what she had to offer wouldn't make them short of breath.

I rebelled. I do sometimes if I've got into a sordid situation following my appetites. I get a sense of my responsibilities. It is really a rebellion on behalf of Tres, Edna and the children—my shareholders. Tres in particular rubbed off on me. I'm more decisive than I ever was before I met her. I switched off the programme. I didn't like this big stone prick or what it stood for so I got my rusty bit of car bumper I was using as a scraper and I pushed the whole bloody thing down.

Diana screamed again. She wasn't underneath or anything. I was only about, what, ten feet up. She was at the bottom of a small hummock of overgrown rock-fall. She ran back to catch the bloody thing as it fell—as though

I'd dropped the baby out of the window. It snapped in the middle on a rock below and that nicely-shaped end broke off and bounced down the hummock as Diana came up. It didn't even appear to hit her; she seemed to stumble on it and then fall backwards over it to land in the grass.

It didn't take me five seconds to get down to her. She lay there on her back in the grass as though she was comfortable. She didn't attempt to sit up but just stared at me.

"Are you all right?" I asked her.

"I think so," she said.

"My rupture went," I said. "I couldn't hold it."

I pushed my fingers into my groin to indicate the pain. She closed her eyes. I have to spell this out. I thought she had closed her eyes because she was angry at my dropping the rock under such a flimsy excuse.

"Honestly," I said.

I sat down by her side and started coaxing her to forgive me. I didn't know it but she had passed out. I never know when people pass out. There's something in me, something cowardly I suppose, which rejects serious accident, unconsciousness and death. I have chatted to somebody paralysed with pain because I've just slammed my car door on their hand. Perhaps I don't look at people enough when I talk to them. Perhaps it's linked with the fact that I don't recognise people I know. Can't describe them. Can't wake them up. Don't know whether they've got a moustache or not.

"We'll find another piece," I told her. I stroked her forehead. It's fatal to start stroking a girl who's lying on her back in the grass in a green satin dress and has been messing you about for five years and using all your bloody petrol. I thought at first she was sulking and after that I didn't give a damn what she was doing.

She doesn't remember it. She doesn't remember it. Thank God for that. I'm so ashamed. She was already paralysed for life. It was like—what's that word when you make love to a corpse? Cedric used to have people do it a lot. Anyway,

I've told you now. I'll be honest. I was going to change this ending, make it a car crash. I couldn't do it. It wouldn't have rung true.

The last thing she remembered, she said, was my saying that my rupture went. That's why I had to go through with my operation.

# 16

# And Others

SANDRA, THE NIGHT SISTER you remember, was overjoyed to find me in the men's ward for my rupture operation. She wangled me a private ward with two beds in it so that she and whichever doctor it was by that time could use the other bed without anybody giving them away. I lost a lot of my sensitivity during the first three weeks and stopped putting my head under the blankets.

"You don't want to go out," she told me one night when I was almost healed. "I never get anybody in I know."

It was another of those rowing-machine nights and I was in there five more weeks with broken stitches and God knows what other complications.

By the time I got out Mary had left the caravan and gone home to await a baby. Whether it was kindness or strategy I don't know but she named Albert as the father and he's probably keeping them.

I didn't see Albert again except in publicity hand-outs and TV interviews but his mother wrote to me at the caravan and asked me if I would take his milk round on until he knew for certain whether or not he would need the job again. It was a silly thing for me to do really because once a freelance writer takes any kind of salaried job the steady wage corrupts his talent; undermines the necessity of selling something before the rent's due. You start thinking about what you'll write next instead of doing it.

In the afternoons I used to go and visit Diana at the Orthopaedic Hospital. I could see what was going to happen when she came out and I made one desperate effort to avoid it by writing to Tres. She didn't want me to go to the Wimbledon flat and instead arranged a meeting at the *Daily Mail* Ideal Homes Exhibition.

We sat in the ideal living room of an ideal split-level house like an ideal family supplied by the manufacturers. People were staring at us and smiling as we tore each other to pieces emotionally. Lewis stood at a therapeutic umpire distance as if giving us a last chance. Fiona played a dreadful tear-jerker on the ideal piano, her crooked eyes seemingly fixed on the bass notes though in fact she was sight-reading.

"I don't want to be stuck for the rest of my life, Tres—I don't even love her."

"You crippled her," Tres said. "You can't desert her as you deserted *our* Diana."

She was giving me another of her penances to do.


Since then I have shouted, telephoned, written urgent letters and telegrams, lit bonfires, usually when stinking drunk. I wrote to a newspaper, a member of the House of Lords and my publisher. They were desperate, raving letters, straight out of a bottle, but they brought only the mildest of replies. The newspaper said my letter was receiving attention, the Earl offered to come to tea with me and my intriguing lady next time he was my way, the publishers misunderstood me:

*Dear Horace* (my publisher wrote),

*Delighted to hear from you at last. Thanks for a sight of the new material. It looks absolutely splendid to me and I'm glad you're taking a little longer this time.*

I wrote to Cedric, explaining my situation here fairly fully and asking if he could lend me enough money to get to Ireland and had he any friends in Dublin who could put me up until I got on my feet. The reply came back from Tres who seems to be seeing quite a lot of him now that she lives and works in London.

*Dear Horace*

*The children and I are alarmed that nothing of yours seems to have appeared anywhere for a long time. For God's sake don't stop putting your writing first now that you've got rid of your responsibilities. Cedric tells me the last thing you sent him was rubbish.*

The last thing I sent him was my letter. Instead of helping he sat down and reviewed it.

I get the afternoons off and I went in to see Cedric and to try to see Albert. I had to make elaborate excuses to Diana about renewing writing connections, trying to make some money so that she can have a motorised invalid car; afterwards for verisimilitude I retailed interviews that I'd had years ago.

I was disappointed and hurt by Cedric's attitude. He had little patience with my troubles but took a morbid writer's interest in my account of my life with Diana; particularly our sex life and the domestic arrangements. He questioned me closely about how I washed and ironed her underclothes.

"You enjoy it, don't you?" he said.

I denied it.

He said: "I'm not sure that this isn't a sublimation, Horace. You never liked sophisticated women—or even women. Unless they were young, helpless, practically terrified, you couldn't do it. You had nervous impotence with normal women. Frankly Horace," he said, in the tone of one friend to another, "I think you've been sickening for a paralysed girl for a long time." He pushed his tooth back

[187]

and rushed on: "You're the kind who rape little children! Except that you're too civilised, kind, rational, humorous—" He kept adding words like that until I sat down again.

Oddly enough I came away with the feeling that underneath it all he was furiously jealous. He gets into these rages in the middle of a normal conversation. I can understand them stoning him. I don't think his home life with Sheila is everything he pretends.

Albert, who has made two pictures (one very successful) since I took over his job on the milk round, was in the restaurant with the titled executive and some colleagues. The commissionaire wouldn't let me go in but was kind enough to take a note in for me. While I was waiting outside I heard somebody calling my name.

"Horace?"

It was the tramp sitting on his sacks in the alley. The one Arturo used to mutter to.

"Sit down, boy," he said.

I sat down with him on the sacks and he gave me a cigar. I never liked cigars but there's a time when if something costs money you'll use it.

"You don't remember me, do you, Horace?" the tramp said.

I told him I did. But he meant before the times I walked up and down with Arturo.

"I'm Ralph," he said.

"Oh my God!" I said. Of course he was Ralph. It was another old gravestone. He was the B-picture man who years ago had first shown me Arturo's office and said one day he would have a place like that.

"I'm sorry," I said.

He wasn't upset or anything.

"You've changed too," the tramp said. "Are you writing anything at the moment?"

He wasn't really interested; it was just that way we have of getting the subject back to what we are doing.

[188]

"I've got a big one ready to go," he said. "They're talking about it now."

He stopped to wave past my shoulder and I looked round. The titled executive and Albert had come out of the restaurant, laughing together, their arms around each other. Their colleagues, over-fed and red with the warmth of the wine followed them out, trying to get their laughs in. They all waved back at us, making sure that we could see them waving, as if it was a superstition and they were afraid they might get struck like us if they didn't wave.

I thought perhaps Albert hadn't got my note; I'd brought a story I wanted him to consider and I'd asked him for my fare home. Then I saw his mother come out of the restaurant with Popsie, the commissionaire pointing me out to them. Mrs Harris came over and gave me half a crown.

"Send the story in, Horace," she said. "He'll get to it as soon as he can."

I called a greeting to Popsie but she pretended not to hear. She's never forgiven me for not burning those papers though she's had two associate producer credits out of Albert.

"They're giving me a decision next Tuesday," Ralph said. Then he said, snapping his fingers: "Have you got a story would suit Elizabeth Taylor?"

I told him about *The Virgin Prostitute*.

"That's been done," he said. "Hasn't that been done?" He pulled out a *Daily Cinema* and scanned it. "No—there you are. That's one of Harris's forthcoming subjects—he took it over with Conti's company."

"That's my story," I said.

"Look," the tramp said, "whenever you put up a story always send a copy through the post to your agent—the date stamp proves your copyright. I always do that. Hello, Queenie."

A street woman had come out from the passage behind us. She was wearing a short black plastic mac, her face painted like a hoarding. I would swear this was the same

[189]

prostitute we picked up in Loughborough; with the same tramp. How strange life can be, gentle reader.

"This is Horace Spurgeon Fenton," he told her.

"Queenie Nightingale Fforbes," the tart said, shaking my hand.

"Two f's," Ralph said. "Sit down, Queenie."

I stood up while she sat down, tucking her legs under her.

"This is really a board meeting," Ralph explained. "Queenie's in this with me. You see it's her true story. It's moving ahead nicely," he informed her. "They wanted to cut my percentage but not me. The co-production deal with the Hungarian studio depends on my contacts—he's the chef at the Troc in fact." He drew luxuriously on his cigar and blew it generously into her face. "We've got them over a barrel, darling," the tramp said.

He asked me if I was available to do a major scene script and I told him that I was, but mentioned the milk round.

"That's no good," Ralph said. "You want to be on the spot. It's the only way."

"Just a minute," Queenie Nightingale Fforbes said. "I think I've got a customer." She got up and followed a man into the passage, turning to call: "Ten minutes."

"I discovered Queenie," Ralph confided. "She was doing bit parts when I met her. I see we're going to get the quota again. . . ."

I left the tramp immersed in his *Daily Cinema*.


I've had one Sunday morning horse-ride with old Angie which finished in the long grass in tears.

"I've never seen you cry before," I told her.

"I know. Did you like it?"

I did and told her so; it joined us as never before though I misunderstood the reason for her distress: her marriage was coming up at Easter.

Wiping her tears with the tail of my shirt, for we can only half-undress, I said: "It's not the end of the world,

[190]

Angie. I shall still see you. When you're married I'll be your milkman."

"I'm not crying for me I'm crying for you, Horace!"

Apparently she was worried about my being free. "You must get Tres back," she said. "You're not fit to cross the road on your own."

"Don't worry about me," I said. "I'll be all right."

"I do worry," she said. "I love you, Horace. I'm the only one who really loves you. You're a fiction man, you should know that."

"Through thick and thin?" I asked. But she was deadly serious:

"Say you love me," she said, as we came up to a climax.

I refused. I don't think it's right unless it's absolutely meant. One day I shall say it.

"Who to?" she cried. "Who to? You're fifty years old, Horace. When's it going to happen?"

She was trying to frighten me; and still further when she remounted her horse. "Horace I don't want to see you any more. I thought you were simply innocent but you're not—you're retarded." She started sounding like Cedric as she rushed on, digging her heels into her horse's flank, trotting away—I could hardly keep up with her. This is when she said: "That girl Diana—that monster you push up and down the High Street—" Funny she should say "Monster" don't you think? "—she's no good to you! You've done it again, Horace! You choose completely the wrong kind of women. Never givers—always takers!" And she started galloping away, her cheeks streaming with tears. They had given me a middle-aged horse and I couldn't keep up.

"Come back!" I shouted, but she didn't. "I love you!" I shouted. "I love you, Angie!"

I don't think she heard me. The last thing she shouted was: "You've got you're freedom, Horace—and now you're chained to it!"

And then she jumped a hedge.

There are worse things than a milkman's job. You appear to be rushing and rattling about but it is such a routine, like changing gears in a car, that it requires no thought. Very often when the round is over I can't remember having done it. It is an ideal job if you want to plan a novel or think up plots. I can understand how Albert came to do all his dreaming.

I have made a lot of friends on the round and I have been unfaithful to Diana's hair several times. I have to go back in the afternoon with eggs, because you can't stop during the round. Most of my conquests have been by courtesy of Albert's goodwill; they remember him and they want to talk about him. A few want to sue him for maintenance, though I usually get them to laugh it off with an anecdote about him. Secretly they are rather proud to have known him, for he's seldom out of the newspapers and when his pictures are shown locally everybody goes. One thing that usually pays off is sending for signed photographs of him for the newly-weds. I can get as many as I like, of course.

I am planning to get my hair cut.

I shall have it done a little at a time so that she doesn't notice what's happening. If the book goes on any kind of scale I shall try to opt out but it will have to be done gradually. I shall need a lot of help and it will have to be paid for.

I shall need money, love, understanding, a bearded long-haired nurse, a rope-ladder and psychiatric treatment. I shall need a fast car and plenty of roads. I shall need a warm, comfortable home with food and drink and cigarettes.

I shall need a girl who will come to bed when I go to bed, go to sleep when I go to sleep, get up when I get up, see me in the morning.